St. Helens Libraries

Please return / renew this item by the last date shown. Items may be renewed by phone and internet.

Telephone: (01744) 676954 or 677822
Email: centrallibrary@sthelens.gov.uk
Online: sthelens.gov.uk/librarycatalogue

E

JF

2 8 JAN 2022

1 5 AUG 2022

Jennifer Killick lives in Uxbridge in a house full of animals and children. She is the author of five epic MG titles with Firefly, including the much-loved *Alex Sparrow* series. Her books have been selected for The Reading Agency's Summer Reading Challenge for four years in a row. The first book in this series, *Crater Lake*, was a *Times* Children's Book of the Week and was selected for the Book Trust Book Buzz programme in 2020. Jennifer loves to visit schools and talk about her books, whether on zoom on in person.

Other books by Jennifer Killick

Alex Sparrow and the Really Big Stink
Alex Sparrow and the Furry Fury
Alex Sparrow and the Zumbie Apocalypse

Mo, Lottie and the Junkers

Crater Lake

CRATER LAKE
EVOLUTION

DON'T. EVER. FALL ASLEEP

First published in 2021
by Firefly Press
25 Gabalfa Road, Llandaff North, Cardiff, CF14 2JJ
www.fireflypress.co.uk

A CIP catalogue record of this book is available from
the British Library.

1 3 5 7 9 8 6 4 2

Print ISBN 978-1-913102-64-7
Ebook ISBN 978-1-913102-65-4

This book has been published with the support of the
Books Council of Wales.

Typeset by: Elaine Sharples

Printed by CPI Group (UK) Ltd, Croydon, Surrey, CR0 4YY

JENNIFER KILLICK

CRATER LAKE EVOLUTION

DON'T, EVER, FALL ASLEEP

Firefly

For the old new friends that
I feel lucky to have in my life:
Lorraine Gregory
Eloise Williams
Bruce, Cian and Rhys

Contents

1
Battle Royale

'Die, loser! Die!' Chets' voice screams through my headset as he pulls off a 360 no-scope with the majesty of a leaping panther.

'Is that your thirteenth kill, Chets? What happened? Bandito9000 has turned into a savage!'

'My time as an alien wasp changed me, Lance. You don't experience something like that without growing from it. I think it activated some dormant skills that I never knew I had.'

'Gaming was literally the only thing I was better at than you.' I groan as I take a hit. 'Do you have a med kit?'

'On my way, StarshottA51,' Chets says. It's so good to hear his voice. 'And you're amazing at lots of things.'

Standard Chets, trying to be kind, when we both know it's not true. 'Yeah, I'm amazing at doing lousy in tests, getting detention and making my mum stress.'

'Is she in the hospital today?'

'No, actually.' I am frantically building to get some height so I can kill some dude called RabidMilson2006 who is apparently desperate to get me out of the game. 'She's home. She seems better.'

'That's great, Lance,' Chets says, as Bandito9000 effortlessly takes down RabidMilson2006, leaving me looking like a noob.

'Thanks, mate,' I say. 'She's been so ill since our Crater Lake Year Six school trip-slash-fight for survival in the summer that I'd forgotten what it was like to have normal Mum around the house. She's smiling and singing again. It's nice.'

'It wasn't your fault, you know,' Chets says.

'Feels like it was.'

Mum's illness can get triggered by stress, and let's just say that what happened at Crater Lake made her lose her mind with worry. You can't blame her, really. She thought she was sending me on a Year Six residential where the scariest thing that would happen would be a bad zip-wire landing, or falling out of a canoe. Nobody expected Crater Lake activity centre to be the HQ for an alien takeover.

There's just us and two other duos left in the game.

'None of us asked for it to happen, and if it wasn't for you, we'd all be creepy bug creatures.' He pauses and I swear I can hear him shudder at the same time I do. 'Like Digger. How are you sleeping now? Any better?'

Sleep has never come easily to me, and it's been even worse since Crater Lake. The crater contained the remains of a meteorite which released invisible spores into the air. Sleeping at Crater Lake allowed the spores to use your body as a host, turning you into an alien slave. When sleep means the end of your life as you know it, it becomes the enemy. And that's not a fear you get over easily. The CPAP oxygen machine I use every night helps with my sleep apnoea, but it doesn't take away the nightmares.

'You know, same as usual,' I say, because I don't want sympathy. We've all struggled with awful memories of our residential.

We take out another team.

'You'll always be a hero, Lance,' Chets says. 'No

matter what happens, you'll always be the one who saved us.'

As much as I'd love to take all the credit – the respect I got after defeating the alien hordes and stopping them from taking over the world was the high point of my life so far, and I will almost definitely never get that kind of glory again – winning at Crater Lake was a team effort. Everyone had courage, and everyone had skills. Chets with his smarts and tech genius; Kat with her kindness and insane talent for climbing; Mak with his prepper survival knowledge and bear-like strength; and Ade with her mega-brain and super-speed.

'We all saved each other, Chets. You, Katja, Mak, Ade and me.' I glance at the screen. 'They're not coming, are they?'

'They might still,' Chets says. 'They're probably just running late.'

'VenomAde has joined another party.'

'Is Adrianne still hanging out with that new group? The ruffians?'

I smile. Only Chets would use a word like ruffians. 'Yep. She's so different now.'

'And she and Katja haven't made up yet?'

I glance at the screen. No sign of xKittyGrimeX. No texts from Kat on my phone.

'They haven't spoken to each other for months. And when I tried to talk to Kat about it, she got so mad that she won't speak to me anymore either.'

'Do you miss her?' Chets asks.

Like the polar bears miss their melted icecaps.

'Nah. Well, maybe a little, sometimes.'

'I always thought you two would end up…'

I fake a coughing fit to hide my pain. I know he's trying to help, but I really don't want to hear this right now. My screen turns red. *You were eliminated by UglyPugly1985.* 'Sorry, Bandito,' I say. 'I suck today.'

'It doesn't matter, Lance. It's just a game.' He says this, but I can hear the frustration in his voice. He's become way more competitive lately, and Chets hates doing badly at anything. Not that he did badly – I totally dragged him down with my lameness.

'You'd have been better off with MakKarnage,' I say. 'But I think we've lost Mak for good.'

'You never know. Nobody can predict these things, especially those of us who are inexperienced in matters of the heart.'

In spite of everything, I splutter out a laugh.

'He got his ear pierced,' I say. 'I'm not sure there's any way back from that.'

'Is it golden, like a pirate's?'

'It's a giant diamond. It sparkles in the light so you can see him twinkling from the other end of the corridor.'

'That sounds kinda nice, in a way. Festive.'

'I'd love to agree with you, Chets, but it's more like the Poundland version of Ronaldo. And it just doesn't seem like, you know, Mak.'

Chets takes a slurp of drink. 'I guess they really aren't joining the party. I used to love it when we all played together every week.'

'Me too.' For a long time it was literally the only thing I looked forward to. We promised we'd carry on the tradition: every week, no matter what. 'I guess everything changes, even if we don't want it to.'

'True say,' Chets sighs, and I smile at that.

'As they aren't coming,' I say, as carefully as I can, even though I know saying it carefully probably isn't going to make a difference. 'Would it be OK if I invite my other friend, FreshTrim?'

One, two seconds of silence.

'Chets?'

'Which friend do you mean?' he says. He knows which friend I mean.

'FreshTrim101, my friend from school: Karim. I told you about him a couple of times, remember? He moved to Straybridge over the summer because his parents are working on the SMARTtown project. He didn't know anyone when he started at Latham High.'

'I vaguely recall you mentioned a new ... acquaintance.'

Talking like he's got something painful stuck up his butt. He gets like this every time I try to introduce him to Karim.

'You'll really like him, Chets – he's a good guy. He's funny.'

'I'm sure he's hilarious,' Chets says. 'But I think it sends the wrong message to have him in our party, just in case the others do show up. We don't want them to think they've been replaced.'

'No, we don't,' I say. 'But having a new friend doesn't mean anyone's been replaced. It's just a new friend.'

'Hey!' Chets says. 'I've just thought of another thing you're the best at. You always win at wing roulette, because you're the only person I know who can handle the extra hot without crying.'

'Well yeah, that does make me a bit of a legend,' I say, knowing there's no point in pushing any harder. I don't want to lose Chets on top of all of the others. 'Duos again?'

'For sure, StarshottA51. Let's go.'

As we haul out, ready to parachute into another game, a tap on my shoulder makes me jump out of my skin.

'Jeez, Mum!'

'I was calling you for ages. I wish you wouldn't have that on so loud – you're probably damaging your ears.' She ignores my eye roll. 'After this game, I want you to come and decorate the Christmas tree with me. It's been sad and bare for far too long.'

'Who is sad and bare?' Chets says into my ear.

'The Christmas tree,' I say. 'Because apparently trees have feelings, too.'

'Hi Chets!' Mum shouts into my ear, and waves for some unknown reason.

'He can't see you, Mum,' I say.

'Hi, Mrs Sparshott,' Chets shouts back.

'Should I just give Mum the headset so you two

can chat?' I say, and then, 'Joking, Mum!' when she reaches out to take it. 'I'll come down in ten, OK?'

'If you don't, I'll come up again.' Mum laughs and finally leaves my room.

'Why haven't you decorated your tree?' Chets says.

'It was delivered a week ago and Mum felt too unwell to do it,' I say. 'But apparently now she's feeling better enough to hang some baubles, and ruin my life by trying to chat to my mates.' I am a bit embarrassed, but it's so good to have her joking around that I'm actually quite looking forward to doing the tree with her.

'Right. Ready to drop in three, two, one...'

And then a boom thunders through the house, so loud that I hear it clearly over the game. So loud that the walls shake. The spare oxygen canisters for my CPAP rattle and clink together for a few seconds, and then go still.

'Did you hear that?' Chets says, as I jump out of my gaming chair, which is hard cos it's really low, and I'm slightly lacking in core body strength. I dart to the window, forgetting that I'm attached to my console by the headset lead. It jerks me back, and my headset thuds onto the carpet, at the same time as my mum runs back into the room.

Outside my window, the winter sky is the palest grey-blue, quiet and clear without even a bird to break up the view. I can see a way across Straybridge, beyond the shopping mall and the church in the town centre, and across to the other side of town, where a plume of black smoke is billowing into the air.

I fumble my headset back on as my mum gapes open-mouthed at the scene outside. 'You seeing this, Chets?'

'If you mean the apocalyptic toxic cloud, then yeah, I'm seeing it.'

'I'm going to look at the news,' Mum says, heading downstairs. 'You stay here.'

I grab my phone and start scrolling through social media. Within thirty seconds I'm seeing the same word over and over again. Explosion.

'What is happening?' Chets gasps, probably looking at the same feeds as I am.

I stare at the smoke churning and bubbling in the sky above my town: a town where literally nothing interesting ever happens, and I feel a creeping dread prickling in my chest.

'I don't know,' I say. 'But, to use the words of every great *Star Wars* hero, I have a really bad feeling about this.'

2
Old Enemy

It only takes a minute for the shocked silence to be replaced by the sound of sirens. I watch from my window as distant blue lights zip down streets towards the smoke, and I'm trying to work out exactly where they're going. It's got to be a couple of kilometres away, which means the explosion must have been big for both me and Chets to hear it from our houses.

'Lance, I've got to go,' Chets says. 'My mum is having a meltdown.'

'Yeah, no problem, mate,' I say, my mind still racing as I try to work out what could have happened. 'I hope she's OK. Text you later.'

'Let me know if you find anything out,' Chets says. 'See ya.'

I pull off my headset and scroll through my phone again.

'Lance! Come downstairs, will you?' Mum shouts up. 'Something's coming on the news.'

I jog downstairs to the den where Mum is sitting on the sofa with the remote control in her hand.

'*We are interrupting our programming to bring you a breaking news story,*' the newsreader says. '*There have been reports of a large explosion in the town of Straybridge. The cause is not yet known and we have no details of any casualties. Local police and fire services are responding to the incident and we're hoping we can provide you with more information shortly.*'

'What is happening, Lance?' Mum whispers, and I can see that she's scared. This is not good for her.

'I don't know, Mum,' I say. 'But it might not be as bad as it looks.'

She pats the sofa next to her, and I perch on the edge of the seat.

'*The explosion is believed to have originated at the university campus in Straybridge.*'

'Oh god, I hope Nadia's OK.' Mum grabs her phone with shaking hands, and holds it up to activate her face ID. 'Stupid thing,' she shouts when it fails to recognise her three times because she's moving around too much.

'Here,' I say, taking it from her and holding it up to her face to unlock it. 'And I'm sure she's OK. It's Saturday, so she'll be at home with Karim.'

Mum scrolls through her recent calls and then puts the phone to her ear. 'Damn, it's engaged!'

'I'll call Karim.' Mum is going into full-on panic. Since she met Nadia at the hospital back in June, they've become really good friends. And I'm glad because it was our mums who introduced us before we started at Latham. I really didn't want to meet Karim at first, because it was weird being set up by our mums like some kind of arranged friendship. Plus I already had my mates and I wasn't looking to add any more. But we got on as soon as we met. We have loads in common and have a laugh. And, as it turned out, my other mates didn't last that long into the first term.

'Sparshott, my G!' Karim's voice shouts into my ear. 'Can you believe what is happening?'

'Is your mum OK?' I say, because Mum is literally whacking me on my knee and mouthing words urgently in my face.

'Yeah, we were all at home when it happened,' Karim says. 'Mum's just gone in now to try to find out what's going on.'

14

'She's fine, Mum,' I say. 'She's just gone in now to try to find out what's going on.'

'Oh, thank goodness,' Mum sighs. 'Tell Karim to tell his mum to call me when she gets a chance.'

'Did you hear that, K?'

'Yep. Will do.'

I give my mum a nod, and then shuffle back on the sofa while she goes off to make a cup of tea. 'So, what do you know?'

'Not much, really. Just that there was some kind of accident at the lab that caused an explosion. Mum went nuts, got on her phone and went off in the car.'

'It was definitely an accident?' I ask. 'Someone didn't blow up the lab on purpose?'

'She seemed to think it was an accident, but we don't know anything for sure. She was mostly worried about the possibility of experiments in the labs being compromised.'

'What sort of experiments?' I ask. I've never really wondered what goes on in there before, but it suddenly occurs to me that maybe I should have.

'They have a few different departments,' Karim says. 'Obviously she mostly works on the XGen stuff so she doesn't know much about what happens in the other areas. Why? What are you thinking?'

'I'm not sure,' I say. 'I guess I'm wondering if there was anything dangerous in the labs.'

'So you're thinking the town is going to be overrun with those creepy pink-eyed rabbits, spreading zombie germs through the population? You've been in too many life-or-death situations, my friend – you've gone straight to disaster movie mode.'

'Yeah, I guess.' I lower my voice so Mum won't hear. 'I just know that there are things out there in the universe that are dangerous. I don't want to get taken by surprise again.' Karim has heard all about Crater Lake, so he knows where I'm coming from.

'Dude, it is so unlikely that anything like that would happen here. The only thing that Straybridge is known for is all the SMARTtown stuff – renewable energy and super-fast wifi. If I was an alien species, intent on destroying the human race, this is the last place I'd start. Besides, didn't those spore things come out of a meteor hole or something?'

'Yeah,' I laugh. 'They came out of a meteor hole.'

'Well, I haven't seen any meteor holes around here, have you?'

'No, I haven't … but maybe there was something in the labs. I just want to be ready.'

'Lance Sparshott, you were born ready. You are the readiest person I know. I have been secretly calling you "Mister Ready" since I met you.'

'Alright, I hear you,' I say. 'Talk later?'

'I'll call you when I hear from Mum,' Karim says. 'Be ready.'

'I will.'

'I know you will.'

I laugh and hang up as Mum comes back into the room, looking a lot less upset than she did before. 'Shall we decorate the tree now?'

'Sure,' I say. Nothing like something getting blown up to make you feel festive. 'Shall I get the boxes down from the loft?'

'No need,' she beams. 'I've already done it.'

'Mum,' I say, 'that wasn't smart – what if you'd fainted?'

'But I don't feel faint. I can't remember feeling this well for ages. I'm not tired, I can eat normally,

17

and there's no pain. Plus, I'm sure my hair is getting shinier. Does it look shinier to you?'

I look at Mum's long, dark hair and honestly, I have no idea. Who thinks about how shiny their mum's hair is? No one, that's who.

'Yeah, I think it is. Definitely.'

Mum pulls the boxes of decorations in and we begin to unpack them, untangling lights and pulling off layers of bubble wrap. The TV is still showing the news, but they're mostly boring on about all the SMARTtown stuff.

'Straybridge won a competition to become the country's first SMARTtown as part of a new scheme, receiving a huge financial investment in the areas of science and technology. Benefits to the town include solar panelling on all houses, and the opportunity to be the first place in the country to trial XGen's cutting-edge phone and data services...'

Blah, blah, blah.

'Isn't the tree lovely?' Mum says, smiling at it like it's her favourite child.

'It's very tree-ish,' I say, glancing up at it. 'And big.'

'It's one of the special ones from Verge's Garden Centre,' she carries on, regardless of my lack of interest. 'You know they dig them up leaving enough of a root ball that they are still living, and can be replanted after Christmas. Isn't that incredible?'

'A living tree? Sure. Mind blowing.'

'So they continue to produce oxygen. It was one of the things that helped us to win the SMARTtown investment.'

'The cones on it are a weird shape,' I say, reaching out to inspect one of them. It's wider and rounder than normal pinecones, and the petal-slash-scale things are bigger, so it sort of looks like a rosebud made out of wood.

'They're special, aren't they? They'll begin to open up in a few days – the smell is supposed to be divine. Have you found the end of those lights yet?'

'Yep.' I pass it to her. Mum is a total weirdo about the decoration placement, so I mostly just pass her things while she puts them on the tree. Apparently, there is an exact right place for each one.

'*We have just received an update from the Straybridge police. They aren't allowing anyone, reporters included, into the town. Anyone not within the town's boundaries at this moment is being told to stay away.*'

We both look up to see images on the screen of police setting up roadblocks and turning cars around.

'Why would they do that?' Mum says, her arm frozen midway to hanging a crystal butterfly on a high branch.

'Maybe they don't think it was an accident, and they want to catch the person who did it.'

'Then they wouldn't be letting people out, but you'd think they'd still be letting people in. This doesn't feel right.'

'It's OK, Mum. They're probably just being careful. We'll find out more soon.'

She nods and carries on with the decorating, but I can tell she's anxious. The newsreader is interviewing 'experts' and they're all guessing about what might be going on, which isn't helping. And I know I'm reassuring her, but inside I am reeling and sweating and trying not to show it. Not saying I'm an expert on danger, although that would be like the most cool job to have, but I am certain in my bones that something is seriously up. Trouble has always followed me around.

On the surface, we spend the day decorating, eating, and talking about boring same-old stuff, like how Mum always has the heating on too high, and how the cat's been acting strange, but really we're just waiting. We keep the TV on, but with no reporters allowed into Straybridge, there aren't many updates. We see some phone footage of the university straight after the explosion. It's shocking to see the smoke up close, and bits of debris scattered in the air and on the ground. You can hear screaming. There's no blood or anything, though, or people who look hurt. And you can bet that if there were injured people wandering around, someone would have filmed it and put it on social media. So I'm hopeful that everyone's alright.

It's not until late in the afternoon that we finally get some more news. We've just turned off the big light and lit up the tree.

'We're interrupting the afternoon movie with a breaking story from the town of Straybridge,' the newsreader says. 'As you may be aware, there was an explosion in the town this morning that was believed to have originated from the university. We have just been advised that the Mayor of Straybridge, the Chief of Straybridge police and the *communications officer of the SMARTtown project will be giving a statement in just a moment.'*

'Sounds serious,' Mum says, and we sit on the sofa, surrounded by empty boxes and unused tinsel. Mum has a spatter of glitter on her nose. The image on the screen changes to a shot of the mayor standing in front of a wooden stand with the town's crest on it. On one side of him is a woman in police uniform, and on the other is Karim's mum. They look nervous.

'Good afternoon,' the mayor says. *'We have some urgent information to pass on, so I'll get straight to the point.'* He clears his throat. *'This morning, an incident occurred in the research department of the university, which led to an explosion on a significant scale. Fortunately, there appear to have been no injuries or casualties resulting from this explosion. However, it caused severe damage to the Cake building, and the laboratories within.'* He swallows. *'Straybridge University is home to one of the leading scientific research departments in the country – something that we are extremely proud of, and that led to us being awarded the first major grant in the SMARTtown initiative. There is always a variety of*

research projects taking place within the laboratories, and some of these involve living test subjects.' He shuffles behind the wooden stand and I see a trickle of sweat slide down his forehead. *'It appears that one of the test subjects is currently unaccounted for, and we believe that it has fled through the damaged building and into the community.'*

Mum gasps.

'We are in the process of conducting a search and retrieve operation across the town so that we can secure the creature in question as a matter of urgency. In order to prevent the creature from fleeing further, we have created a temporary perimeter around Straybridge. Nobody may enter or leave the town until the test subject has been apprehended. According to my scientific advisor, the test subject will hide during daylight hours, and only be active at night, so residents of Straybridge may go about their daily business without concern. However, though we are confident that the creature does not pose much of a threat, we are introducing a curfew to the entire town, starting immediately. All residents must be inside their homes before sunset, and remain there throughout the night for

their own safety. *Straybridge police will be patrolling the streets to ensure the curfew is respected, and of course to look for the test subject.*

The chief of police lifts her chin, and gives a small nod. This is probably the most action she's had in her life.

'I'll now hand over to Carol Barnes, head of Straybridge Police, who will give you some more details about the new security arrangements.'

He steps back from the stand, and swaps places with Carol.

'Thank you, Lord Mayor,' she says. *'First of all, I would like to reiterate the mayor's message that we do not believe the public are at risk. Our scientific advisor, who is well aware of the behaviours of this test subject, has assured us that the creature won't cause physical harm to people, unless it is attacked. As such, there is no need to panic, or do anything other than to be alert and notify us if you notice anything that might assist us in the search for the test subject. The curfew is a precautionary measure, but nevertheless, an important one. The bells of St Anthony's church will ring a twenty-minute warning in the afternoon, so that residents can return to their homes. The bells will then ring a*

second time, which will be a confirmation that everyone in Straybridge must be inside. Anyone caught breaking the curfew will be subject to a penalty fine, or even arrest. More importantly, those who choose to break the curfew will be risking the safety and security of our town, and preventing those working to protect it from doing their jobs. To be clear: when you hear the church bells, you must go home. Once you're at home, you must stay there until you hear the church bells ring in the morning. If we work together, we are confident that the test subject will be secured in a short time.'

My phone buzzes, and I glance down to see a text from Karim. *'Told ya, the bunneeeez are coming!'*

I text back, *'Lol, when you hear the chimes of doom, you better run...'*

'Ooh, I think Nadia is going to speak now,' Mum says. 'Doesn't she look beautiful? And after the day she must have had.'

I text Karim again. *'My mum is crushing on your mum.'*

He sends me back the tilted laughing, crying emoji.

'Thank you,' Karim's mum says. *'My name is*

Nadia Amrani, and I am the lead communications officer for XGen's Straybridge SMARTtown project. Given the seriousness of the current situation, I wanted to provide some reassurance regarding the SMARTtown project status. Straybridge has poured an enormous amount of hard work into the project over the past six months and, though the cause of the explosion remains unclear at this point, I am certain that it was not due to any fault or failing in the XGen technology. Safety has always been, and always will be, of paramount importance to XGen, and we will be working with the relevant departments to fully investigate what caused the incident. We do not envisage there being any lasting detrimental effect to the project, which will continue after this slight delay. We will, of course, be here to listen to concerns and answer as many questions as we can over the coming days, but for now we must focus on the primary objective of securing the test subject and the laboratories.' She looks around the room. 'Are there any questions?' She nods at an unseen person. 'Please go ahead.'

A voice calls out clearly across the room, and it makes me go cold, cos it sounds so familiar. It can't be, though. It can't be her.

'Will the scientific advisor be available to answer questions about the escaped test subject?' she says. 'The information you have provided is too vague for the people of Straybridge to be able to prepare and protect themselves.'

'The scientific advisor is not available,' Karim's mum says. 'I'm sure you'll appreciate that his time is better spent working to resolve the situation than answering questions about it. But, let me assure you again, there is no reason to panic. The test subject will be inclined to hide during the day, and as such will pose no threat to the public. As long as we all respect the rules of the curfew, I have been assured that we will be safe.'

'I'm sure the public would all feel far happier to hear this from the expert,' the unseen question-asker says. And I'm straining my ears to listen, because I need to know if it's her. 'Will he be answering questions in due course?'

To be fair to Karim's mum, she doesn't drop her calm.

'As I said, Vanya, the scientific advisor is busy working on retrieval of the test subject and the investigation at the labs. I will be sure to relay your concerns to him, and we will issue a statement if *we have any further information that we can share.'*

Vanya. I don't think I ever knew her first name, but there must be someone I can ask who knows it. Teachers' first names and outside-of-school lives are like your parents' social-media accounts: you don't go poking around in them, because you're not gonna like what you see. But I need to know.

'Mum?' I say. She's still staring at the TV, eyes wide, mouth open, listening to the newsreader basically repeating everything that was said at the briefing.

'Yes, babe?' she says, patting my knee without turning from the screen.

'That person who asked the questions about the scientific advisor ... I think Karim's mum called her Vanya. Her voice sounded familiar.'

'It would – she used to be your teacher at Montmorency. She left, after ... well, after your residential, and started working at the local newspaper. I bumped into her once when she was covering a story at the hospital.'

My heart drops in my chest, like when you go to pick up something that's way heavier than it looks, and you go down like a loser, and everyone laughs. That's how it feels – like the universe is cracking up at my expense, throwing the person I hate the most back into my life when it's already being ripped up in a hurricane of explosions and pink-eyed bunnies.

'I can't remember her last name,' Mum says, oblivious to my inner rage. 'Oh, it's on the tip of my tongue.'

I chew my lip and swallow. My mouth tastes like dirt, and saying it out loud isn't going to make that any better. 'It's Hoche.'

3
Glitch

We go to bed late, after checking the doors and windows are locked about a million times. Plus I have to stuff old pillowcases and towels into any potential cracks or openings around the house, including the fan vents in the bathrooms and the tiny gap where the side door isn't quite straight in its frame. Mum wants me to board up the fireplace, Sellotape the plugs into the plug holes and nail down the toilet lids, but I finally manage to persuade her that's a step too far. The cat flap is locked, and only opens when Betty pushes on it cos she has a special fob attached to her collar. We have a mental conversation about whether the test creature would go to the trouble of stealing Betty's fob, just so it could get into our house, and agree that's unlikely.

It's mid December, so you'd think it wouldn't be so bad being sealed into a house with literally no air getting in or out, but Mum has always felt the cold more than normal people, so the central heating is blasting into every room. Apparently, even though she's feeling much better in every single other way, the being freezing all the time thing still stands. My room is so hot it takes me back to summer in Crater Lake, when we were in as much danger of dying from heat and dehydration as we were from the alien invasion. It was the hottest week ever, and since the killer bugs liked everything toasty, they'd made sure the air con was switched off, and the heating was full on.

I stand at my window and peek out between the slats in the blind. The street outside is chillingly quiet – no distant hum of traffic or occasional song from a neighbour coming back from the pub. I've never heard this much quiet, or at least I've never noticed it before. I can't even hear any birds. I watch for movement – a rustling hedge or shadow slinking behind a garden wall. But there's nothing.

My phone pings suddenly, making me jump like an idiot.

It's Chets. *'Mum's making us all sleep in the same bed together. My life is officially the worst.'*

'Oh, mate! No words.' I reply.

'Pray for me. Talk tomorrow?'

'Fo sho. Night. Enjoy your snuggle.'

'Oh man! I hate my life!'

In spite of everything I laugh quietly while I set up my CPAP. My mum's a stress-head, but she's not as bad as Chets' mum. I check everything on the CPAP is attached correctly. I've been using it for most of my life, so the routine is drilled into me. I don't reckon I'm going to sleep much, but if there's one thing Crater Lake taught me, it's that you've got to get what you can, while you can, and that definitely includes sleep.

I put on the mask, checking the seal is secure, and turn on the machine as I lie back on my bed – on top of the duvet because my mum's a maniac and I'm roasting. The CPAP whirrs and I close my eyes as I breathe in the oxygen, trying my hardest not to think about everything that's happened today: the explosion, the escaped test subject and hearing Hoche's voice. I fail, obviously, cos I'm full of adrenalin and halfway ready to grab a weapon and go walking the streets, searching for answers. Sometimes the hardest thing is doing nothing. I don't feel it coming but, at some point, I drift off.

I jolt awake, feeling like I'm falling, my heart thudding in my chest. This is nothing new, so I go with it, trying to slow and deepen my breaths, sucking in the oxygen like it's, well, oxygen. Which you literally need to live. My pillowcase is soaked where I've sweated so much, and my hair is plastered flat against my head. Once my breathing has calmed, I turn off my CPAP and remove the mask. My phone says it's 3:58 a.m. which is not a fun time to be awake. I need cold, so I go to the bathroom and splash icy water on my face. Outside our house it's silent, but my skin prickles when I hear a noise downstairs. The kettle.

'Chill, Lance. It's just your mum,' I say. 'Unless the escaped creature is making itself a cup of tea.' I go downstairs quietly, just in case, and head for the kitchen. The light is off, which is weird, cos Mum's jumpy in the dark at the best of times, and this is pretty much the opposite of the best of times. In the dim light coming from our kettle, which lights up as it's boiling, I see my mum standing over a mug.

'Mum,' I say, turning the kitchen light on. 'What are you doing?'

'Hey sweetheart.' She looks up at me, blinking

33

as her eyes adjust. 'I couldn't sleep, so I thought I'd make a warm drink. Do you want one?'

'Thanks, but I'll probably get something from the fridge, seeing as it's a million degrees in here. Why didn't you turn the light on?'

'I'm not sure,' she frowns. 'I didn't think to, I could see well enough. Probably still not fully awake.' The kettle is bubbling away now, getting louder and steamier as we both watch it. Something feels off, but I'm not sure what. I side-eye my mum as she leans close to the kettle. She looks normal. Well, she looks less ill than normal, but I can't see anything else different about her. I jump again as the kettle boils and its switch flicks up.

'I was hoping Betty might come in for some food,' Mum says. 'I know she's coming home each night, because her food bowl is empty every morning, but she's only darting in and out, and never staying long enough for a cuddle.'

'She's always been a psycho cat, Mum,' I say, opening the fridge and taking out the milk. 'She doesn't let anyone near her except you.'

I wouldn't say Betty and I are good mates, but I like to think we respect each other. We both give each other space to go about our business and have a healthy lack of trust in other people. Unlike Betty, I don't try to rip people's faces off if they get too close. I'd quite like to sometimes, though.

'I miss her cuddles,' says Mum. 'I hope she's not poorly.' She rubs at her arms in the way she always does when she's worried. There have been times when she's left bruises. She picks up the kettle and starts pouring the hot water into her mug. And then something changes. There's a faint sound all around us – so small and high pitched that I'm not sure if I'm imagining it. It lasts for two or three seconds and then stops, and once it's gone, everything seems even quieter than before. I don't know exactly how, but there's a void where something used to be. It sounds mad, I know.

'Did you hear that, Mum?' I say.

She doesn't answer; just keeps pouring. Her body is still, her eyes fixed on something I can't see – an invisible spot in the air. Her mug fills and starts to overflow, water sloshing over the rim and all over the kitchen counter. But she keeps pouring.

'Mum!' I shout, watching the boiling liquid splash onto her dressing gown. It's really thick and fluffy, so should protect her from being burned, but some spatters up into her face and she doesn't react. Not even a flinch. She just keeps pouring. I put down the milk and cross the kitchen as fast as I can. As I reach her, the water from the kettle trickles to a stop. Completely empty. And yet she carries on holding and tilting, not even noticing that there's nothing coming out.

'Mum,' I say, gently trying to take the kettle from her hand. Her grip is solid. I can't even move a finger. She doesn't look at me. I wonder if she's sleepwalking or having a seizure. I'm panicking, wondering whether to call an ambulance, or if I should get her to lie down. I've taken care of Mum when she's ill a million times, but nothing like this has ever happened before. And then she blinks, looks at me, then down at the watery mess she's made. She puts down the kettle and picks up a tea towel.

'Go back to bed, Lance,' she says. 'I'll get this cleaned up.'

'But…' What the hell is going on? 'Are you OK?'

She smiles at me. 'I'm fine. You know how clumsy I can be. I'll sort this out while you go and get some sleep. You look tired.'

'I'm not tired,' I say, grabbing a kitchen roll and ripping off some sheets. 'I'll help.'

She tilts her head and looks at me, and there's something in the way she does it that makes my skin crawl. It's such a small thing, but I'm closer to my mum than anyone, and I know her like I know myself. This isn't her. This is new.

There's a scratch at the back door, and for what feels like the hundredth time today, I physically jump, and my already rocketing heartbeat moves up another notch. Betty jumps in through the cat flap onto the kitchen tiles. She looks up at us and skids to a stop. Then she fixes her eyes on Mum, arches her back and hisses like a demon cat. I look from her to Mum – Mum who loves this cat more than almost anything else in the world; Mum who was fretting about her just a moment ago.

'Interesting,' Mum says.

I swallow. Take a breath. 'Why's she growling at you?'

'Who knows?' Mum smiles. 'But you said yourself that she's always been a psycho cat. I'm sure she'll get over it.' And she goes back to mopping up the spilt water.

Betty turns and disappears back out of the cat flap at lightning speed, leaving it swinging behind her.

'I'll finish here,' Mum says. 'You really should go up to bed.'

'OK,' I say, suddenly wanting to be as far away from Mum as possible so I can think. 'I'll go and lie down.'

She stops wiping, and smiles again. I try to look at her eyes without looking like I'm looking at her eyes, and it makes me sick to think about it, but I know what I'm expecting to see: black – lots of black, like an alien worker; or even worse, the yellow rings of a bug-eyed hunter. But they're the usual brown. If she's been body-snatched, there's nothing to show it.

'Night, Mum,' I say, realising that there's not actually much left of the night now. Maybe an hour or two until the church bells ring, and then I can get out of this house. I turn and walk, as calmly as I can, back up to my room, my mind spinning totally out of control. I don't know what's happened, but I need to make sense of it. There's one thing I am sure of, though: whatever that thing was in the kitchen, it definitely wasn't my mum.

4
Kat

I don't go back to sleep. I sit in my room going over everything I know, trying to add it all up into something that makes sense. Obviously my thoughts turn to Crater Lake, and I wonder if it's possible that something nasty followed us home from that awful place. There are similarities – my mum's sudden personality transplant being the main one – that make me think it's a possibility. But how could she have been infected by alien spores? And if she has, is she a worker or a hunter? At Crater Lake there were two kinds of alien enemy – the workers who were mindless drones, working away at jobs to help the swarm; and the hunters, who took charge of the workers, and of turning all humans into bug-eyes. Her actions in the kitchen last night didn't fit either type. There's also the matter of her eyes, which looked reassuringly human. All I can come up with are questions and more questions, so it's clear to me what I need to do next.

I stay up in my room until the church bells ring, then I make a break for it, sneaking down the stairs and towards the front porch. When I bend down to put my trainers on, there's not a sound in the house, so it's yet another jump-scare when my mum's voice rings out, way closer to me than she should have been able to get without me noticing.

'I hope you're not going out, Lance. We should be at home together today.'

I keep tying my laces. Don't look up. 'But you're feeling so much better, Mum. And I really want to go check on the cat.'

'The cat is used to being outside. It will be fine.' She's standing at the porch door now.

'I just want to make sure,' I say, standing up and pulling my coat off the hook. I risk a glance at Mum: she still looks normal, apart from the unfamiliar expression on her face. I look down at my fingers, willing them not to shake while I do up the zip. I need her to think everything's fine.

'The best place for you is right here.' Mum stands her ground. 'Safe at home, tucked up away from any danger.'

Weird thing to say. Very weird. I need to get out of this house.

She steps forward and puts her hand on my arm.

'I couldn't get back to sleep last night,' I say, 'because I was worried about Betty. Finding her will put my mind at rest, and then maybe I'll be able to catch up tonight.' I reach for the door handle and edge slightly away from her. Her hand stays on my arm, her grip tightening. 'I could really use a good sleep, but I don't think I'll get one until I know she's OK.'

She tilts her head like she did in the kitchen. Pauses. 'Perhaps it will be for the best, then, if it will help you sleep.' She lifts her hand from my sleeve, and I notice my coat almost clinging to her skin, like her palm is sticky. I pretend not to notice as she pulls a little and it peels away, making a soft tearing sound, like velcro. 'Make sure you're back before curfew.'

'Of course,' I say. 'Have a good day, Mum.' That's it: handle down, door open, and I'm out. I look back to see Mum watching me, so I give her what I hope looks like a carefree wave, then I turn on to Honeycroft Road and break into a run.

'Later, Betty,' I call, as I pass her curled up snoring under a hedge. I know I should stop to see if she's alright, but I have more important things to worry about. This is all about as bad as it could be and I'm gonna need back-up.

When I get to the house, my courage falls like a pound coin out of a pocket hole. I stare at the door a bit, nudge forward to knock, and then change my mind. I thought this would be easy, but now that I'm here, I realise it's more frightening than facing down a whole swarm of alien nasties. I chew my bottom lip, and go to knock at least three more times before the door suddenly opens of its own accord.

'What are you doing, Lance?' Kat says. 'You've been out here for twenty minutes.'

She's looking at me like I'm a straight-up lunatic, but all I can see are those eyes, the colour of cartoon dolphins leaping gracefully out of sparkling ocean waves.

'Hi Kat. I came to see you.' Lame. So lame.

'But you decided you'd rather look at my front door instead?'

'I … wasn't sure you'd be happy about me being here. Things haven't been great between us. Obviously.'

'So why did you come?' She opens the door a

bit wider, and her frown softens a bit. It's like she's trying to stay mad at me, but her anger is weakening. I sense this is an important moment. If I get it wrong, she'll never talk to me again, but if I get it right, I'll have my friend back. I decide the best play is to be honest.

'Something's wrong, Kat,' I say. 'In this town, and with my mum. I was hoping you'd help me to find out what. It would mean a lot.'

I'm dying of cringe, so I look at my trainers which, I realise, are busy scuffing up Kat's mum's paving stone with a sharp-edged pebble. I'm swearily cursing at myself in my head and kicking the pebble away, so I don't notice Kat moving towards me. I feel it before I see it – a rush of warmth, and Kat's arms around me, hugging me like she hasn't since the summer. I feel my whole body relax with relief, and I hug her back, breathing in the smell of her, which is like Christmas cookies fresh out of the oven.

'I've missed you,' she says into the side of my head. (She's a few centimetres taller than me.)

'Yeah, I've missed you, too,' I say, hoping desperately that I don't start crying. 'I'm so glad you don't hate me.'

She steps back and looks at me, her breath coming out in fluffs of white steam, like perfect, magical clouds. 'I could never hate you, Lance. How could you think that?'

'Er, because you said, "I hate you, Lance Sparshott. Never talk to me again."'

She giggles. 'Oh yeah. Sorry – I was really upset. I didn't mean it. Well, I did at the time, but I got over it after a few weeks.'

'Why didn't you say?' The thought of us not talking when we could have been talking is almost worse than the thought of us not talking because she hated me.

'I thought you hated me because I'd been so horrid. And none of it was your fault – it was between me and Ade.'

'Everyone gets mad, and does things they wish they could take back, Kat. I know that better than anyone. There's literally nothing you could do that would make me hate you.'

She makes a face like she's trying not to cry. It's cute – like a piglet with an itchy nose or something. 'Same,' she says.

'So we're cool, then?'

'Always.'

And, just like that my world gets a million times better, even with all the beef that's going on.

'Come in for a bit,' Katja says, pulling me inside. 'We've got so much to talk about.'

'Is everyone ... normal in your house?' I ask, looking down the narrow hallway towards Kat's living room.

'As normal as they usually are,' Kat says. 'Eva's still asleep, but she never gets up till about one, and Mum's gone over to Granny's to check on her, because of the phones.'

'What about the phones?' I say, as Kat's cockapoo, Nugget, comes bombing down the stairs and leaps on me, tail wagging like crazy.

'How can you not know?' Kat says. 'Get down, Nugget!'

Nugget is awesome. I give him a hug and let him lick my ear, even though it's gross, cos it's such a relief, firstly that I'm here with Kat, and secondly that her dog isn't freaked out like my cat is. 'It's OK,' I say. 'I've missed Nugget too.'

'It's like ten a.m. and you haven't even checked your phone yet? You're a disgrace to our generation.'

'Honestly, I couldn't think about anything this

morning except the mental stuff happening in my house.'

'Sounds like we need snacks. Let's get snacks.'

I follow Kat into her kitchen, with Nugget bouncing around at my feet.

'Drink?'

'Anything with caffeine, please.'

'Crisps or cake? Actually, I'll get both.'

I lean against the kitchen counter while she gets a tray of stuff together, then I carry it into the living room which is about as Christmassy as it's possible for a room to be. About a third of the room is taken up by the derpiest tree I've ever seen. It's only a bit taller than Katja, but it is about three times as fat as it is high. It has loads of thick branches on one side, and hardly any on the other, with just a few jutting out here and there. It's leaning over like it's trying to find a white feather in the snow. 'Wow,' I say.

'Isn't she beautiful?' Kat beams. 'I love her so much.'

'You chose it on purpose, didn't you?' I put the tray down on the coffee table, being extra careful not to spill anything. I already scraped up Kat's front path, I really don't want to stain her carpet, too.

'Of course. I like to choose the special Christmas trees that look like they really need a loving home.'

'It's definitely, erm, special,' I say, and Kat whacks me in the arm.

'So, the phones,' she says. 'We woke up this morning, and nothing was working. No phone signal, no internet. Nothing.'

I pull my phone out of my pocket. It's fully charged but has zero bars of signal. I try to get onto social media, but it won't connect.

'It's the same from our laptop,' Kat says. 'So we took Nugget for a walk and spoke to some other people in the park, and they all said theirs aren't working either.' She slurps some tea. 'The word among the dogwalkers is that the XGen stuff caused the explosion at the university and now their network has gone down.'

'If that was true, surely the network would have gone down when the explosion happened?' I say. 'But it was fine yesterday.'

'Good point. It definitely went off overnight. Maybe something else happened at the lab.'

I think back to the moment my mum glitched into freakishly terrifying mode. 'I need to know

47

the exact time it switched off,' I say. 'Something weird happened to my mum last night, and I know it sounds insane, but I've got a feeling they're connected.'

'What happened to your mum?' Kat puts her mug down and puts her hand on my hand.

'It's hard to explain. She was standing in the kitchen, making a cup of tea, and then she sort of stopped. It was like her body was there but her mind was reloading, or buffering or something. And then, when she finally restarted, she was ... different.'

'Different how?'

'It was like she was someone else. Like she'd been hypnotised, or body-snatched.'

Kat's eyes widen, and I know she's thinking the same thing that I'm thinking. Anyone who'd been at Crater Lake would jump straight to the alien-spore takeover explanation, because when you've been through something like that, it stays with you and changes the way you see the world forever.

'She looked the same,' I say. 'Her eyes were normal, and she didn't spit any sedative slime at me, like you'd expect a bug-eye to do. But she was acting differently, for sure.'

'Did she have a worker or hunter vibe?'

'No. This was something else – something in between.'

'So maybe she hasn't been spored? How would there even be spores in Straybridge?'

I use my not-being-held-by-Kat hand to pick up my mug and take a big gulp of tea. 'I don't know. But Betty went full psycho when she came in from outside and saw Mum. And have you noticed there's no bird noise in town?'

'Oh god, you're right,' Kat says. 'About the birds. I'd noticed something was missing, but couldn't figure out what. I thought I was suffering from wifi withdrawal.'

'The birds always seem to be one step ahead,' I say. 'They'd left Crater Lake before we even got there.'

'And now they've left town.'

'There's another thing,' I say. 'Mum's really keen on the idea of me going to sleep.' Now that I'm saying all this out loud, I'm even more sure that I'm right. I take a breath. Try to calm myself. 'I think something other than us made it out of that crater.'

5
Karim

We finish our snacks and head out into town. We need answers, and the obvious place to look is at the university. But we need to pick up someone on the way.

Karim lives in a three-storey house on the new estate just outside the town centre. We can't call or text to tell him we're coming, but I'm basically his only mate, so I can't think of anywhere he'd be other than at home. It's about a fifteen-minute walk from Kat's to Karim's, and it's so good being with just Kat that I honestly almost wish it was further.

'You're sure he's going to be OK with all this?' Kat says, as we walk up to Karim's front door.

'He knows everything that happened at Crater Lake and he's cool with it.'

'I don't mean this in a horrible way, but knowing about Crater Lake and seeing it with

50

your own eyes are really different things. I'm not sure I would really understand it if I hadn't been there myself.'

'I hear you,' I say. 'But we've got really close and I genuinely think he can deal.'

'OK then,' Kat nods. 'Let's ring the bell.'

I hesitate, wondering if she has a problem with him. She goes to Latham so she knows who he is and that he sometimes gets in a bit of trouble. 'I know he messes around at school, but he's a good guy. I really think you'll like him.'

'If you like him, I know I will too. You're a good judge of character, Lance. You always have been. Ring it.'

Shouldn't have doubted her.

I press the doorbell and we watch through the frosted panes as a figure comes to the door. In the distorted glass, he doesn't look human – his head twice the size it should be.

'That hair, though,' whispers Kat, as the door opens.

'Sparshott!' Karim says. 'Have you come to protect me from the pink-eyed devils?'

'Huh?' Kat says.

'Oh, hey,' Karim says, noticing Kat and

immediately pulling out the big smile with the deep dimples (he's majorly proud of them). 'It's Katja, isn't it? I don't think we've ever been properly introduced. Damn shame.'

'Hi Karim,' Katja smiles back. 'It's nice to meet you.'

I'm not even slightly comfortable with this bit of flirting, so I get straight down to business. 'Is your mum home? We need to ask her something.'

'Not what I was expecting you to say, but if you need to know whether this is natural,' he runs a hand across his massive bush of curly hair, 'I can assure you that it is one hundred per cent pure Karim.'

Kat snorts out a laugh and Karim flashes the dimples again.

'It's about XGen,' I say, in a way that makes it clear that this is a time for decisive action and not for being charming and funny. 'We need to know what time the network went down and if she knows how it happened.'

'Right.' Karim drops the grin. 'She's gone to the university to – in her words – "find out what the fudge is going on". They weren't her actual words but you get the idea. We could go down there and find her?'

'Yes,' I say. 'Let's do that.'

'Come in for a sec while I make myself fly.'

'We were just gonna walk, but sure if you want to get there before us,' I say, cos I don't want Kat to say that he already looks great, which is the kind of thing she'd say because she's always nice to people.

Kat giggles, which makes me feel better.

'You can make your jokes, but I'll have the last laugh, mate, because I actually do have a super power.' Karim makes putting a hoody on seem like the hardest thing in the world as he tries to get it over his head without messing up his hair.

'What is it then?' Kat says.

'My hair, obviously. One day it will save the world.' He looks in the mirror and frowns. 'But not looking like this. One minute.'

We follow him down the hall and into the cosy room we spend most of our time in when I'm at his house. I like it in here – there's a two-seater sofa with a fleecy blanket over it, the squashiest chair I've ever sat in, a big screen TV with his console hooked up and a few shelves of books. In the far corner is the Christmas tree – the only decoration they have in the house – and on the wall next to it is a massive mirror, which Karim looks in multiple times whenever he walks past. That's where he goes now, with a can of hairspray in his hand.

'I like your baby Christmas tree,' Kat says, gently jingling a little gold bell on one of the branches and leaning in to sniff a pinecone.

'We're not that big on Christmas, so we only get a small one,' Karim says, spraying his hair like he's spray painting a car, or maybe a whole house.

'Sure you've got enough there, mate?' I say, trying not to choke on the fumes.

'Not yet,' he says, giving it one last blast. 'Now I've got enough. Let's go.'

He grabs the pouch he carries everywhere with him, and a minute later we're out the door and heading across town towards the university.

'You are messing with me,' Karim says, when I fill him in on what happened with my mum. 'That is some crazy shiz. You must be losing your mind.'

And it's funny, cos a part of me is freaking out, but the bigger part of me feels calm, like I've been waiting for this for the past six months. 'Actually, mate, I feel ready.'

'Of course you do. You're Lance Sparshott – you were born ready.'

'Aw!' Katja says. 'Do you two have a special thing that you say to each other? Is this your thing? It is so cute!'

'We do not have a thing,' I say, and I nudge her with my elbow.

'Woah, Lance – you're breaking my heart!' Karim says. 'We totally have a thing.'

We're all laughing hard, and I notice a postman watching at us as he empties a postbox. I stare him down, but he doesn't look away.

'He's not the only one,' Karim says, nodding at the postman. 'About ninety per cent of the people of Straybridge have been gazing adoringly at us since we left my house.'

'Seriously?' Kat says. 'I didn't notice anything.'

'Me neither.' I glance to my right to see a face at a house window following us with its eyes.

'Oh, you two didn't notice? I wonder why...' Karim says. 'At first I thought it was because of my good looks, but after the twentieth person, I started thinking that maybe there's something else going on.'

I look across the other side of the street where a

woman is putting a black bag in her wheelie bin. In an upstairs window, two blonde-haired toddlers sit with their toy dolls. A flower delivery van crawls past, windows down, a woman in dungarees with bright red hair not concentrating on the road. They're all staring at us.

'Well, this is creepy,' Kat says.

'Totally.' My mind flicks through the possibilities, but we just don't know enough to be sure of anything. I decide our best play is to act as though nothing has changed. 'Let's just pretend like everything's normal. Our only advantage is that they think we don't know what's going on.'

'Hate to be a buzzkill, but we really don't know what's going on,' Karim says.

'But we know that *something* is going on,' says Kat.

'And that's not nothing.' I smile and nod at the wheelie bin lady. 'Let's hope we can get some answers from your mum.'

We keep our pace steady as we walk, resisting the urge to break into a run or to hide from all the randoms looking at us like we're meat on a stick. The strange thing is that, what with it being freezing cold and just before Christmas, you'd think people would be either tucked up at home, or out shopping. But it's like there's been an alert to tell everyone in town to stop what they're doing and watch us.

'Do you remember this time yesterday when the world hadn't turned into a scene from a really bad dream?' I say. 'Seems like ages ago.'

'What do you think the creature is?' Kat says. 'The one that escaped from the labs.'

'I've been thinking about that.' I shove my hands deeper in my pockets, wishing I had some gloves. 'I reckon it's one of three things. Either there is no escaped test subject, and it was just an excuse to keep us all shut inside at night...'

'But why would they want us to be shut in at night?' Karim asks.

'So someone can be up to something around Straybridge without anyone seeing,' I say. 'Or...'

'The sleep thing.' Kat blows out a breath, the vapour swirling like a ghost in the air.

'Well, that's sinister,' Karim says. 'What's option three?'

'That the escaped test subject is something so terrifying they can't tell anyone what it is.'

'So even worse, then. Cool, cool, cool.'

We turn on to Falling Lane and I see the university campus looming above the trees. It's a massive place – buildings of different shapes and sizes spread over a huge area, with the River Brink running through it. The central high street type area is paved and ramped, so I've been skateboarding here a few times during the holidays when all the students have gone back home. It's pretty dead now, though I see a few twitching blinds as people look out at us.

'Mum will be at the Cake,' Karim says, pointing at a building over the other side of the river. It's enormous and white, and circular and layered, which is why people call it the Cake. In the past few months, masts have been added to the top of the building. They reach up into the sky, probably ten metres or so, and are covered in shoebox-sized futuristic glass cylinders that light up at night. So, the Cake became a birthday cake when XGen moved in. Right now, it's surrounded by a police barrier, at least five security guards and a butt-loads of uniformed police officers.

'That's a lot of security,' Kat says. 'How are we going to get in?'

'We'll think of something. Let's check it out.'

As we approach the Cake, every pair of eyes is on us. I can see a huge blackened area on the centre right of the building and loads of broken windows. There's debris scattered everywhere, and neon-numbered markers placed here and there, like you see on those forensics shows.

'Right,' Karim says, smoothing his eyebrows for some reason. 'Leave this to me.' He heads straight towards the main entrance, swagging up to the doors like he owns the place, and makes to walk past the four police officers standing either side of it. They immediately move to block his way in.

'What up, my Gs?' Karim says, giving them the dimples.

'This is never going to work, is it?' Kat whispers as we slowly follow.

'Not a chance. We'd better start thinking up a plan B.'

Karim seems to not be put off by the seriously hostile looks being shot his way. 'My mum works here,' he says. 'And she wanted me to come and collect something from her.'

'No one gets into the building,' one of the police officers says. 'At all costs.'

'I should mention that she basically runs the

place,' Karim carries on. 'So it's completely cool for me to be here. I'm always allowed in.'

'Go home,' angry police guy says.

Kat and I watch as Karim tries to argue his way in, even though it clearly isn't happening. He tries everything: guilt trip, puppy eyes, threats, but they're having none of it. I'm just about to go and get him so that we can regroup, when a sound behind me makes the hair on the back of my neck jump up like it's just seen a sign for free V-bucks. The click-clack of high heels on concrete echoes around the campus, cracking through the quiet like gun shots. And, to be honest, they might as well have been for the fear that surges through me as I listen to them getting closer.

'Oh god,' Kat whispers. 'Those are footsteps I hoped never to hear walking towards me again.'

I take a breath. 'Hoche.'

6
Spatter

We both turn to see Miss Hoche powering up to us, and a guy with a video camera scurrying along a couple of metres back. She's dressed up smart, with a long belted coat over a dress, and a purple scarf around her neck. Her shoes are purple too, with pointed toes that look just ripe for kicking someone somewhere painful. That someone probably being me.

'Lance Sparshott,' she says, stopping a few paces away from me. 'How inevitable to encounter you at the scene of a crime.'

'Miss Hoche,' I say, gritting my teeth.

'I wouldn't be surprised if it was you who caused the explosion – arson and vandalism are likely to be the only skills you possess.'

Still a vile witch, then. 'Are you gonna give me a sticker for that? Oh, wait – you can't. Because you're not my teacher anymore.'

61

One corner of her mouth twitches upward in the start of a nasty smile, and she tilts her head to the side in a way that makes me shudder. 'I was never your teacher. It's not possible to teach a child like you: a child incapable of learning or achieving anything worthwhile.'

Karim jogs over to us. 'Those guys aren't human. None of my good stuff worked.' He looks up at Hoche and raises a now-unsmoothed-again eyebrow.

'This is Miss Hoche,' Kat says.

'*The* Miss Hoche?' He makes a face. 'I've heard lots about you, Miss Hoche. All good things, obviously.'

There's a moment of awkward silence.

'Is there a reason you're here – somewhere you have no business being – other than to cause trouble?' Her eyes don't have the alien yellow rings of a hunter anymore, but they still make me feel cold.

'My mum works here, actually,' Karim says. 'For XGen. She's communications officer on the SMARTtown project.'

'So she caused the explosion in the lab, set free a dangerous test animal and shut down the network so that we can't communicate with anyone outside of Straybridge? It makes sense that a friend of Lance's would come from a criminal background.'

God, I hate her.

'Hey!' Karim says. 'My mum didn't do any of those things – she's trying to fix them.'

'She's in charge of XGen commuciations, and now we have a service blackout – that's rather too much of a coincidence, don't you think?' She turns sharply to the camera guy. 'Get this on film.'

He fumbles with the camera and points it at us.

'Where was your mother – the communications officer for XGen – at four a.m. this morning? Was she here at XGen's Straybridge headquarters?'

'No, she was at home in bed like a normal human.' Karim's angry now.

'And where were you, Lance Sparshott, when the network went down?'

'I was at home, in the kitchen, with my mum,' I say, my brain ticking over Hoche's questions. 'And how is four a.m. significant?'

'You really aren't very intelligent, are you?' Hoche sneers at me. 'The network went down at four a.m. I was researching on my laptop when I lost access to the internet, and all connectivity disappeared. Very convenient for XGen to be able to stop me from looking into what they were really doing here at the university.'

'Why would Karim's mum damage her own project?' I say.

'To silence me. To shut the world out. To protect a secret.' She's shouting now, and a bit of her spit lands on my face. I try not to puke.

A movement and voices at the entrance make us all turn to look. A man is coming out, surrounded by security people who are so freaking enormous that all I can see is a flash of his hair.

'Move,' Hoche barks at her camera dude, and she click-clacks towards the doors, barging into security and trying to push her way through. There's a shout from the guards and she stumbles and falls to the ground at their feet. Suddenly what must be every police officer in the university and surrounding area appear from between buildings and through all the entrances and exits, and come sprinting towards her. They are saying something as they run that I can't make out. I don't wait to find out what it is.

'This is our chance,' I say, and Kat and Karim follow as I run around the side of the building.

'There,' I say, pointing to a fire exit about two thirds of the way around the Cake.

'But they only open from the inside,' Karim says. 'Unless you have secret Hulk powers, I don't see how we're getting in that exit.'

'Leave that to Kat,' I say. 'Katja, will you do the honours?'

'On it.' She ties her hair back in a ponytail as she runs to the wall next to the fire exit and looks up. Two floors above is a window that must have had all of its glass blown out in the explosion. Kat pushes off from the floor and grabs on to one of the white metal poles that form the building's exterior structure. It's an impressive jump – she must get about two metres of air. She swings from one arm for a second, then pulls herself up so that she has another handhold and her feet are on the wall. Then she darts up the building like she's never done anything easier in her life.

'Oh, I see.' Karim gazes up at her. 'You don't need secret Hulk powers, because Kat has secret Spider-Man powers.'

I grin as Kat disappears through the open

window. We hang back against the fire exit door, keeping a look out for any police or security, but Miss Hoche's unintended distraction was a good one, and a few minutes later Kat opens the door.

We're in a dim, narrow corridor that looks like it doesn't get used very often. There's a cleaning cart parked against one wall, and a few broken chairs piled up next to it. Kat leads us forward and through a door to the bottom of a stairwell.

'Where will your mum be?' I ask, as we start up the stairs.

'Probably her office – third floor.' Karim looks up as the lights flicker on. 'The building's laid out like a wheel, with spokes leading off the main hub. I usually use the lift, which is right in the centre.' He stops to catch his breath. 'Lifts are great, aren't they?'

'Come on.' Kat bounds ahead. 'We don't know how long we'll have before someone catches us.'

We climb to floor three as quickly and quietly as we can, passing nobody and not hearing any signs of life. The door creaks as Kat pushes it open, and we come out of the stairs into a wide, bright corridor with high white ceilings, and glass-fronted offices along each side. A lot of the glass is cracked or shattered and the whole place stinks of smoke.

'Lucky it's Sunday,' I say. 'There's no way we'd be able to get through without being seen if there were people here.'

'If we follow the corridor, we should end up at the hub. I'll be able to find Mum's office from there,' Karim says, breaking into a jog. I guess with everything that's happened, he's starting to stress.

It's only when we reach the central hub that I can appreciate the massive scale of the building. 'Woah,' I say, my voice bouncing around the huge space. We're standing on a balcony that runs in a circle, with the spokes of corridors running off all the way around. A glass barrier stands between us and a long drop to the marble floor below. It's circular – maybe twenty metres across. Our faces are level with the top of the tallest Christmas tree I've ever seen – taller than the one in the town centre even. Most of its baubles are smashed on the floor below, but the tree is upright and in one piece. Above us is a glass roof, cracks splintering across it like a spider's web, and through it I can see the metal and glass masts on top of the building stretching upwards.

'This way.' Karim turns left along the balcony and then left again into a corridor.

Kat gives me a look, and I know she's as worried as I am about what we're going to find. We turn into the corridor to see Karim disappearing into one of the offices. He shout-swears and there's a thud that sounds like he's booted something. We skid into the room and almost plough into him. He's standing, breathing heavily, his face in his hands.

'What is it?' Kat goes straight to him and puts a gentle hand on his shoulder, while I look around. Unlike the other offices, Karim's mum's has clearly been tidied up after the explosion. The bin contains the pieces of a broken plant pot, and the books that must have fallen from the shelf have been piled up by the desk. Something on the floor by Karim's feet catches my eye: some dark, splattered drops that are soaking into the rug.

'That's not coffee,' Karim says, looking at it through the gaps between his fingers. I crouch down for a better look. He's right – it isn't coffee.

'Is it...?' Kat asks.

'I think so,' I say. 'I think it's blood. I wish Mak was here – he'd know for sure.' I grab a tissue from a box on the desk and dab one of the spots with it, watching the red liquid seep into the white paper. 'It's still wet,' I say.

'So she's probably still here somewhere, and she's hurt.' Karim looks up. 'We have to find her.'

'Just wait one moment, man,' I say. 'I know you're worried, but we need to think before we run into trouble. This might not be as bad as it looks.'

'Blood spatter is never ever a good thing,' Karim says. 'Like never ever.'

'Fair point,' I say. 'But we can only help your mum if we stay calm.'

'Lance is right,' Kat says. 'That's only a tiny amount of blood – if your mum was seriously hurt, you'd think there would be a lot more.'

'Like it would be up the walls,' I nod. 'This is more like a minor cut amount. Also, we should look for clues – does anything seem different to you?'

'It all looks like it usually does,' Karim says. 'Apart from that hoody – that's not my mum's.'

I pick up the hoody that's hanging over the back of the desk chair. It's a kind of faded dark-blue colour, with a small logo on the front –

which looks like the turret of a castle. 'I know I've seen this logo before,' I say. 'But I can't remember where.' It's there in my brain somewhere – I know it is, but I can't quite get at it. 'What a bad time not to be able to Google.' There's another thing, too. 'Smell this,' I say, handing the hoody to Kat. She lifts it to her nose and cautiously sniffs.

'What is that?' she says. 'It's not like any body spray I've ever smelt.'

'Here, let me.' Karim grabs it. 'I'm an expert on grooming products.' He inhales deeply and frowns. 'Unless there's a new flavour of Lynx I don't know about, I have no idea what it could be.'

'It's really sweet,' Kat says. 'But not in a nice way.'

I put the hoody back on the chair, quick as I can, not wanting the smell to rub off on me, but then pick it up again and check the front pocket. Inside there's a plain plastic card with a magnetic strip across the back. I don't know if it's anything important, but I put it in my pocket anyway, and take one last glance around the room. In the middle of the ceiling is what looks like a metal spider, about the size of an upturned cereal bowl.

'Looks like they have a sprinkler system,' I say. 'Weird that it didn't go off in the explosion.'

'Can we look for my mum now?' Karim says.

'Course,' I say, thinking about what I'd do with an injured woman if I was a human/bug hybrid and wanted to take over the world. 'The more I think about it, the more I'm sure that if a bug did take her, they'd want her alive and in good shape. The bug-eyes need every human body they can get. Plus, she has loads of information about the town, she's got a powerful job, and she has connections to the people in charge. They'll want to use her.'

'You mean they'll want to turn her,' Karim says, looking like he might cry.

I don't want to freak him out, but there's no point in lying to him. There's nothing worse than being told everything's OK when you know that it isn't, even when it's said with the best intentions in the world. When you know the reality of a situation, you can start dealing with it, and dealing is definitely what we need to do here.

'Yeah, I think they'll want to turn her.' I look him in the eye. 'But there's a way back from that. We know: we've done it before.'

'You brought your friend Chets back, right?' Karim says.

'Yes. And, if anything, the whole being a host to an alien spore thing actually helped him.'

'It's true,' Kat nods. 'He's so much more confident now. And Miss Hoche who you met outside – she was a really nasty bug-eye.'

'And now she's back to her really nasty semi-human self,' I say. 'Unless she's been re-infected and is involved in all this.'

'Hard to tell,' says Kat.

'Because there's still too much we don't know. But we have an opportunity here to get some answers. We might never get back into this building again, so we need to find out what we can about the explosion, and what they were keeping in those labs.'

'Definitely up for sneaking into a restricted area,' Karim says. 'And I bet that's where Mum is.' He jogs out of the office.

'Where are the labs?' Kat says as we catch up and keep pace with him.

'The only place that a bunch of creepy-ass labs could be,' Karim says. 'The basement.'

7
The Labs

At the far side of the hub is a shiny white door with a yellow and black restricted access sign displayed across it. It's guarded by a chrome keypad – of course it is – so I start to run through any possible ways of getting in. We're exposed in the hub – nowhere to hide if anyone comes in the main entrance or up one of the spokes. We don't have much time.

'Stand aside,' Karim says, cracking his knuckles. 'I got this.' He types a code into the keypad and surprisingly the light turns green. He grins. 'I know all of Mum's passwords.'

'Legend,' I say.

'I'm glad you think so, because I know all of yours, too.' He pushes the door and jogs off.

'His hair must be full of secrets,' Kat whispers, following him.

We're in front of a lift with another restricted

access sign above it, along with a sign pointing to the stairs.

'Lift?' Karim asks, with the sweet optimism of an alien apocalypse noob.

'Stairs,' I say. 'Using the lift could give our location away.'

'It's a very quiet lift,' Karim says, but follows me through the door to the stairwell. The stairs to the basement are the metal kind, with gaps between each step that make you worry you're gonna fall right through. They also clang every time our feet land, and I grit my teeth at every thud.

'We're doing a lot of jogging today,' Karim puffs, his pouch bumping against his side as we descend. 'I hate jogging.'

'I love jogging,' Kat says. 'I always think of it like friendly running – you get to places fast but you don't have the burning lungs.'

'Speak for yourself, Spider-Girl. My lungs are burning plenty.'

'How far down does this go?' I say, peering down the stairwell.

'Far,' says Karim. 'I did mention the lift for that reason.'

'Let's hope nobody else is down there, or we're

going to have to get back up these stairs at faster than jogging speed.'

'If that happens…' Karim wipes his forehead with his sleeve. 'You'll have to leave me behind.'

We finally reach the bottom of the stairs, and exit the stairwell into a large rectangular hallway totally covered in polished chrome. There are two restricted access doors set into the wall in front of us, like steel sentinels standing between us and the labs, and, hopefully, some of the answers we need. The door on the left has a gleaming XGen sign attached to it, so we head there first. Karim manages to crack the code without too much trouble, and I'm wondering if I should be more careful about accessing anything private in front of him from now on. The door slides open with a swish, and we step into an area lit by the blueish light coming from a bank of about twenty monitors that cover the whole of the far right wall, all showing error messages.

'I guess Mum didn't have a chance to get XGen back on.' Karim runs over to the monitors and peers at a screen. The bright ceiling lights flicker on, leaving us exposed in the open-plan room. 'Weird, cos this error is basic. I reckon even I could fix it.'

'Maybe we should do it?' Kat says. 'It would be good to have some wifi right now.'

'I'd need a bit of time, which we don't have,' Karim says. 'Plus, we'd need to get onto the roof and reboot the masts.'

The XGen area is huge, with desks set up in groups of four, and a chest-height counter running all the way around three of the walls, covered in equipment that looks like the kind of thing you'd expect to find in NASA. The furthest wall has doors leading to separate office cubicles. Everything is silver and white.

'It's like being inside a fridge,' I say. 'We're way too visible – we need to be quick.'

'More jogging,' Karim says, starting forwards up the central aisle, towards the office doors. It's the only place his mum could be.

'I wonder what all this equipment does.' Kat gazes around at the piles of science stuff. 'Scientists aren't very tidy, are they?'

'One of the rooms at the end is a clean area,' Karim says. 'But the rest of this place is like the inside of a hoarder's garage.'

I scan the area as well as I can, noticing that there's a sprinkler system down here, the same as up in the Cake, and that it clearly hasn't gone off. There are no signs of damage caused by the explosion, apart from a few things on the floor, including some of the XGen signal beacons that we all have attached to our houses.

'The beacons didn't smash when they fell off the counter,' I say, surprised because they have what looks like a cylindrical glass casing around them.

'It's not normal glass,' Karim says, over his shoulder, as I stop to poke one with the toe of my trainer. 'It's practically unbreakable.'

'Did they use the same stuff on the masts?' I say, but Karim is too far ahead to hear.

It's about sixty metres to the other end of the room and the doors of destiny. One of them is glass and leads to the clean room through a kind of glass pod like an airlock. We can clearly see that there's nobody in there, and as much as I'd like to go in and look around, we don't have time.

We try each of the other doors, but all we find are rooms full of stuff.

'There's no one here,' I say, as Karim starts peering under desks and inside drawers, though I don't know how he thinks his mum's going to be inside one of them unless she's been chopped into tiny pieces. 'We need to move on.'

Karim swears and nods, and we head out of the XGen labs, leaving the light to flick back off behind us.

'We're trying the other secret lab, right?' Kat says.

'I don't think I can get into this one.' Karim looks at the security pad next to the middle door. 'They're not XGen, so I doubt my mum's codes will work.'

'Who uses them, if it's not XGen?' Kat crinkles her nose like a cute baby hedgehog. 'There are no signs on them.'

'There are loads of other research projects going on here, not just XGen stuff.' Karim tries stabbing a few numbers into the keypad. 'Mum says some of them are like top-secret government ventures that only a handful of people know about.'

'Is your mum supposed to tell you stuff like that?' Kat says.

'She doesn't.' Karim smiles, then frowns as the keypad lights up red. 'She doesn't tell me anything, but I make it my business to know. Eyes and ears, friends. Eyes and ears.'

'What's that slot on the side of it?' I say, and as soon as I ask the question, I know what it is. I pull the plastic card I found in the hoody out of my jeans and slide it through the slot. The pad lights up green and something in the door clicks.

'Genius,' Karim says. 'Now let's see what's behind door number two.'

8
Lights Out

The room behind the second door is very different from the XGen lab. It's darker for a start, and we're totally blind for the few seconds it takes for the lights to buzz into life. We're standing at the beginning of a corridor with closed metal doors lining each side. While the other offices in the building have name plates on the doors, or friendly looking labels saying 'Boardroom' or 'Storage', the doors here are assigned just numbers and letters.

'This must be the place we need,' Kat whispers. 'It's a bit more Hawkins than the XGen labs.'

'Definitely more of a dungeon vibe,' I say as I walk to the first door. Karim puts his hand on the handle, but hesitates. 'It's like ripping off a plaster,' I say. 'It's gonna hurt either way, so you might as well get it over quick.'

'What if there's a Demogorgon in there?' Kat says.

'If you were keeping a Demogorgon locked up

in an underground lab,' I say, 'you wouldn't keep it in the room nearest the front door. If it got out of its room, it could wait till someone opens the door from outside and force its way through. Or, if it wanted revenge, it would just block the door and murder anyone who tried to leave.'

'Where would you put it, then?' Karim asks.

'Towards the back, in an area that hardly anyone accesses, and with another concealed exit somewhere close by in case things went bad and you had to abandon ship and leave it shut in the lab forever.'

'Will you at least give it a comfy room?' Kat says. 'Poor Demogorgon – no wonder he wants to kill everyone.'

Karim pulls down the handle and swings the door open. It's just a storage room full of empty glass tanks, microscopes and piles of sealed cardboard boxes.

'How could you contain a Demogorgon anyway?' Karim says, as we move to the next room. 'Surely it would just go back to the Upside Down and then reappear somewhere else.'

'Maybe you could find a way to control it,' I say. 'Weaponise it against your enemies.'

'Why can't people just leave the Demogorgons alone? They should be left to roam free in the Upside Down.' Kat pulls the handle of the next door and we peer into a room full of metal shelving, each shelf holding racks of test tubes full of flies. Each test tube is labelled with a code, and the flies ping angrily against the glass from the inside. There's a PC on a desk in one corner, and charts of data stuck up on the wall above it.

'Don't like this room,' Kat says, as we back out and close the door. And I know she's thinking she wants to smash all the test-tubes and set the flies free, but we're all aware that there are bigger things at stake right now.

We make our way down the corridor as fast as we can, opening doors and quickly skimming the rooms before moving on. There's a room that holds floor-to-ceiling fish tanks, each one containing zebra fish. They flit around their tanks, scales shining in the artificial light, and I'd love to know what they're doing there. I wonder if they do. We find another room that's full of food: giant cans of meat and three-litre bottles of fizzy drink are piled up on shelves.

'Lance, look!' Katja gasps, pointing to some

familiar-looking tubs stacked in neat lines along a low shelf.

'Oh man, I could have happily gone through the rest of my life without ever seeing that again.' Since I got back from Crater Lake, I haven't even been able to look at soup. Just the thought of it makes me wanna puke.

'It's their favourite brand and everything,' Kat says.

'That's their favourite brand?' Karim makes a face. 'It's not even Heinz.' And I smile because it makes me think of Chets.

It's when we leave the food room that I start to notice the smell. It's sweet, but not in a nice way.

'This is taking too long,' I say. 'There's some weird shiz in these rooms, but nothing that helps us. I say we head up there.' I nod towards the end of the corridor. The lights in that area haven't come on yet, but I can see that it opens out into a larger room. 'Follow the smell. Agreed?'

'Agreed,' Kat says. 'That smell's not right. Karim?'

'Yeah,' Karim nods. 'Let's do it.'

The lights blink on one by one as we follow the corridor to its end, the smell growing stronger with each step. The space it leads to is about six metres wide and maybe twice that in length, so more like a chubby hallway than a room. There's a glass-fronted lab that wraps around the entire left wall and half of the wall facing us. The glass is undamaged, so I'm guessing it's more of that toughened stuff like the material they used on the signal beacons. The door to it is tinted so that we can't see in, other than through a small circular clear patch, like a porthole. There's a metal pad next to the door, which tells me that we really need to see inside this room.

'Will the card work again?' Kat says, but there's no slot for the card.

'It's biometric.' Karim steps back from the pad and I can see he's right. It has a phone-sized under-lit glass screen with a picture of an eye above it. 'Unless you've got a high-clearance eyeball in your pocket, there's no way we're getting in here.'

Kat, who's the tallest out of the three of us, stands on her toes and peers in through the glass circle. 'So much stuff,' she says, eyeing the room. 'There's a load of silver tables with equipment on them. One of them has some of the signal beacons opened up and laid out, and there are different tools next to them on a tray.'

'And this lab is nothing to do with XGen, right, Karim?' I ask.

'Right,' he says. 'I don't know why they'd be looking at XGen tech.'

'The back wall has charts stuck up on it about human anatomy, and there are images of DNA sequences.' Kat has her head turned at a painful looking angle so that she can get a good view. 'There's a glass container full of yellow goo,' she glances at me. 'I think it's hunter spit. And there's a fish tank inside another fish tank, full of water and green mossy stuff.'

'They're studying tardigrades,' I say. 'Let's hope they haven't worked out how to beat them.'

Kat stands down, rubbing her neck, and rolls her head from side to side. 'I could only see about half the space. There's way more in there, but it's not visible without being inside the room.'

'You did good, Kat,' I say.

'But still no Mum,' Karim sighs.

'There are some labs left,' I say, and we cross to the other end of the hallway, where there's another metal-handled door. I side-eye Karim as we move forward, worrying about how he's doing. This is all new to him, and it's a lot. In twenty-four hours he's dealt with an explosion at his mum's work, the news that there's a dangerous escaped creature in town, and me and Kat turning up on his doorstep to tell him we think there might be an alien incursion starting in Straybridge. We've been watched, snuck into a heavily guarded building, and found what is most likely his mum's blood spatter but not his actual mum who is missing in freaking weird circumstances. Also, he met the horror that is Miss Hoche. He's still standing, but he doesn't look good. I'm scared that what we find behind this door might be too much, but I know there's no turning back now. I open the door.

The smell hits me like a face full of steaming vomit, as warm air pushes out of the dark in front of us. The area ahead is Crater Lake hot – the air thick and heavy, and full of that god-awful sweet smell that we first sniffed on the hoody, ages ago in Karim's mum's office. I remember how quickly I put it down so that the stink of it wouldn't attach to me. Funny. I'm gonna be absorbing it into my pores as soon as I walk through this door. It's darkness ahead, but I'm pretty sure that if I take a step forward, the lights will come on. Just a step into the black and into the stench.

I take the step, breathing through my mouth like a bear, so that I limit how much of the smell enters my nostrils. Then I realise that I'm basically sucking the smell into my mouth instead, and I honestly don't know what's worse. The light sputters on and I can see that we're at the start of a narrow corridor. I can't see how far it goes, or what's at the other end, because of course the lights in this part are only activated when you walk under them. I close the door behind us, flinching as it slams, and try not to think about what could be hiding in the darkness – I guess our talk about Demogorgons has dredged up some bad memories – and focus on what needs to be done. I can only move forward.

We walk single file. Me first, then Kat, then Karim. The stink is making me feel sick, and the dark is unnerving. We only get one light at a time – the bulb behind us gutters out almost before the next one comes on – so we're blind.

'Is it better to be first, or last in these situations?' Karim whispers. 'I seem to remember that the dude at the back always gets picked off first.'

'I think Lance is the most likely to be murdered,'

Kat whispers back. 'We know there's a door behind us, and we'd hear if someone opened it, so we'd know they were coming. But there could be someone waiting, dead still, up ahead, ready to pounce.'

'Or there could be a giant hole in the floor that Lance could just walk into,' says Karim.

'With poison-tipped spikes at the bottom that he gets impaled on,' Kat says.

'Or a trip-wire that activates a high-intensity laser.' Karim again.

'He's sliced into tiny, evenly sized pieces.' Kat.

'No blood because the laser seals each cube of flesh.' Karim.

'We could put him back together, like a Lego person.' Kat.

'Would the pieces interlock, or would we have to glue him?' Karim.

'You guys are sick,' I say, but a snort of laughter comes out with it, and then Kat and Karim are both cracking up.

'Is it me, or is it getting hotter?' I say.

'I hate to say it, mate, but you're getting sweatier, not hotter.' Karim finally stops laughing enough to speak.

'I definitely think hotter,' Kat says, and I'm glad she can't see my face, cos I know it's turning flame red. But then I think she probably just meant hotter as in temperature and I feel stupid for being so happy about the probably-not compliment.

'The ground is sloping down,' I say, to cover up my embarrassment. 'We're going deeper underground.'

'Well, that's always a good sign,' Kat says.

'Totally,' says Karim. 'And this humidity will be making my hair look proper bad.'

'At least it's dark,' I offer. 'And we might not make it out alive.'

'Thanks, man.'

It's hard to estimate how far we've walked, but we must have been following the corridor for about ten minutes when it stops being a corridor and becomes a tunnel. The painted walls become rock, supported by thick wooden beams, and the strip lights become exposed bulbs. The downward slope becomes steeper, the air chewier, and that rotten, sweet stench almost unbearable.

'It feels weird doing this without Mak and Chets,' Kat says.

'Yeah,' I agree. I do wish they were here. Not that I would want them to be in a life/death situation but, you know. And there's someone else missing, too, but though I think of myself as generally quite a courageous guy, I'm way too scared to say her name in front of Kat. We're only just friends again, and the thought of losing that makes me feel more sick than the vomit stink.

'You got me, though,' Karim says. 'And that's good, right?' And he's saying it like he's joking, but I think he's a bit insecure underneath it all.

'For sure,' I say.

'We wouldn't have got this far without you,' Kat says, because she always finds the right thing to say. 'And I'm glad you're here.'

Finally we reach a place that's more like a cave than a room. The walls are uneven rock. There's a water cooler in one corner, next to shelves of giant water bottles, sacks of sugar and boxes of cups. In front of us there are three metal doors set into the wall. Though the walls, floor and ceiling look old and rough, the doors are shiny new and look like they'd withstand a serious battering. They also each have a rectangular hatch, with a shutter fastened down over the top.

'We're gonna look, right?' Karim says.

'Course we're gonna look,' I say, my mouth dry and my palms sweaty. 'But we also need to try not to be seen. So be ready.'

I flip the catch on the hatch on the first door. It slides down smoothly to reveal an opening into the room, striped with steel bars, like a prison cell. I have to stand on my toes to be able to see inside the room, and what I see makes me shudder. It's all white on the inside, and the walls and ceiling are covered with a strange textured material, forming rows and rows of identical bumps like rounded-off plastic pyramids.

'It's sound-proofed,' I say.

'Another good sign,' Karim says.

There's a bench with a mattress laid on it across the far wall, but other than that the room is clear. 'It's set up for someone to be kept here, but it's empty.' I don't know if I'm disappointed or relieved.

'I'll do the next one,' Karim says, opening the hatch and clinging to the rim of it with his fingers so he can pull himself up a bit. And then he calls out, 'Mum!' And it's not his fault, but it's way too loud – the sound bouncing off the walls and echoing around us. I instinctively pull him back and clasp my hand over his mouth, holding it for one, two, three beats before I let go.

He takes a breath. 'Sorry. Can we get her out?'

Kat and I tiptoe to look in the hatch. The room is the same as the last one I checked, but this one has Karim's mum lying on the mattress. My heart sinks when I see her. She has a small cut on her forehead but looks unhurt other than that. The problem is…

'She's asleep,' Kat whispers.

'She doesn't look too bad.' Karim bites on a nail. 'I'm sure she'll be able to walk out of here, if we can just get the door open.'

'Karim,' I say, holding his shoulders and looking him in the eye. 'She's asleep.'

He looks from me to Kat, then back again.

'She might just be resting.'

'I'm sorry, Karim,' Kat says, 'but we're too late. If we wake her up now, things will get a lot worse.'

I see his eyes gloss over. I see him swallow as he tries to compute what's happening and stop himself from crying.

'We can get her back,' I say. 'Like we're going to get my mum back, and everyone else who's been turned. Like we did with Chets.'

'Can't we just try to wake her? She might be OK; we don't know for sure that everyone in Straybridge is being body-snatched by alien spores.'

'After everything we've seen today, you know we can't risk it.' I hold eye contact, waiting to see what he'll do next. Everyone is different, and we all process stuff in our own way. Some people panic, some lash out, some bury their anxiety under a layer of calm. I've only known Karim for a few months, and my gut says he can deal. But, however he's feeling, I can't let him wake her up.

His eyes drop. 'At least I know she's alive and that she's not freaking out.'

'Exactly. Being spored actually makes people physically healthier,' I say. 'Like my mum.'

He nods, and I know he knows that I get it.

'We should take a quick look in the final room, in case there's someone in there who needs help, and then we have to get out of here,' I whisper. 'We've been down here too long, and whoever put your mum here is going to be coming back to check on her.'

We turn back to the hatch, and I glance in as I move to replace the shutter. The bed is empty.

'Where is she?' Kat says as we edge our faces closer to the bars for a better view. There's no sound from inside the cell, just the low electrical hum coming from the cave lights above us. My stomach churns, but whether it's cos of the smell, or the fact that my mate's mum has just disappeared from right in front of us, I don't know. Everything is still and quiet as we stare at that empty bed – so still that the lights flicker off. My nose is poking through the bars in the hatch, my ears straining for any sign that she's in there. And then, at lightning speed, her face appears on the other side of the bars – so close that I feel her breath on my face as she says, 'Who's there?'

We all instinctively hit the ground in less than a second, the movement making the light ping back on. I manage to stop myself from shouting out – god knows how. Kat gasps, and Karim makes a sound like a guinea pig being strangled but there's nothing identifiable. We crouch in front of the door, and my heart is thumping so hard that it actually hurts. I tell myself: *the lights were out; she doesn't know it's us*. The most important thing is that we keep it that way.

'Is someone there?' Her voice calls through the

open grate. 'Please? I need help. I'm being held here against my will.'

Karim's face lights up, and it's honestly gutting to see him like this – there's nothing more cruel than false hope. I reach out to grip his arm at the exact same time that Kat does. I look at him and shake my head, hold a finger to my lips.

'Please?' Karim's mum says again. 'I know there's someone out there. I'm injured and I'm scared – I'm begging you to help me get out of this room.'

Karim frowns, and I think he's OK, but then flash-fast, and before either me or Kat can stop him, he breaks our grip and starts to stand. Time passes in a slow-motion blur as we both reach to grab him. The top of his hair is almost level with the hatch, and if his mum sees it, she'll know it's him. But he stops, raises an arm and slides the shutter upwards, slamming it shut on his mum. There's just enough time for his mum to roar like a raging Demogorgon before he fastens the hatch and stands leaning against the door, breathing heavily.

And then from the room next door – the one we haven't looked in yet, something thuds against

95

the inside of the door. There's no sound, obviously, with the rooms being sound-proofed, but I feel the vibrations of the impact. A second impact makes the door move.

'We have to go,' I jump up. 'Right now.'

Kat and Karim are right behind me as I dart towards the tunnel opening, but then I hear something that makes me swear. Away in the distance there's the slam of a door. More specifically, there's the slam of the door that leads to the tunnel we're standing at the other end of right now.

'Someone's coming,' I say. 'We can't get out.'

9
Dead End

'What are we going to do?' Kat looks at me, and I can see the same fear in her eyes that I'm trying to keep from mine.

Karim is peering up the tunnel, back towards the labs. 'I can't see any light yet, but if they're moving fast, we probably only have a few minutes.'

I try to calm my mind and think. It's just another challenge – there will be a way through it. I scan the cave around us. There are no weapons – nothing we can use to defend ourselves. I consider opening the empty cell and hiding in there, but the chances of them finding us are massive, and all they'll have to do is lock the door and we're done. Our best option is to hide either side of the tunnel entrance until they get here, then try to get around them and run like hell. It's proper risky, but it's looking like we're going to have to go with it.

'Did you hear that noise my mum made?' Karim says. He's pale and sweating. 'She sounded like a fudging monster.'

'Like a Demogorgon,' I say, my brain catching at something. A chance. 'Guys, come and help me move this stuff.'

We run to the shelves of supplies – Kat and Karim taking one end, while I grab the other.

'On three,' I say. 'One, two, three.' And we pull. The shelves are heavy, and the stuff on them even heavier, but we heave as hard as we can. They rock forward slightly, and then the weight of the water bottles takes over the momentum and the whole lot topples forward, crashing onto the ground. In the wall where the shelves had stood, is a door.

'Concealed exit,' I say, jumping towards it and pulling down the bar. 'There had to be one.'

'Legend,' Karim says, jumping over a water bottle as I push the door open.

'Wait,' Kat says. 'Everyone grab a bottle. We can use them to block the door.'

It takes a few seconds, but on balance I think it will buy us more time than it costs, so we pile up a load of stuff against the door, jamming it in as well as we can so that it will be difficult to move. And then we run.

We sprint up the tunnel faster than the lights can turn on, so I almost crash face first into the wall that suddenly looms up in the gloom in front of me. I put my arms up to take the brunt of the impact and grit my teeth as they hit metal rungs.

'Ladder!' I say. 'Kat, you first.'

She's up and off like a squirrel. I shove Karim after her and I take the rear, getting a view of Karim's butt that I never really needed in my life. Lights flicker on as we climb, but for a long time I can't see an end to the ladder. The climbing is hard going. My arms and shoulders are burning with the strain of pulling myself up each rung, and my legs are threatening to go full jelly. Karim is slowing, and I don't blame him, but we need to be out of here before whoever is chasing us gets within spitting distance if we're going to have a chance of getting away without being identified.

'You're nearly at the top,' Kat calls down after forever. 'Just another few metres. There's a hatch.'

At last. AT LAST I see Kat's hand reach down through a circular opening to pull Karim out, and then she grabs me while he tries to get his breath back. I slam down the lid of the hatch and look around me for something to block it with. We're in another storage building, surrounded by crates, and Kat is already pushing a couple to me, ready to slide over the lid. We work together, scraping them across the ground and onto the hatch, then we pull Karim up and move to the shed door.

I open the door a crack so I can peer out and try to work out where we've ended up.

'Where are we?' Karim asks. 'Please tell me it's not somewhere creepy.'

I see a couple of other wooden shed-type buildings, surrounded by hundreds of stone statues – everything from naked ladies to crocodiles. 'We're either in Medusa's lair, or we're at Verge's.'

'What the flip is Verge's?' Karim says.

'It's the garden centre where everyone in Straybridge gets their Christmas trees,' I say.

'They have a really nice café,' adds Kat. 'Best hot chocolate in town.'

'Assuming that most of the people in Straybridge are sporelings,' I say, 'we can't risk being seen by anyone. So we find somewhere nearby to hide out and lie low until things have calmed down.' As much as anything else, we need to rest. Especially Karim – he's not looking too good.

'Where, though?' Kat says. 'They'll be searching for us.'

'Assuming also that there are still some people who aren't sporelings, they can't openly hunt us down in public. They'll have to be careful. If we can find somewhere with good cover, and where we can see people coming, I think we'll be OK.'

'I know a place,' Kat says. 'The stock shed. Follow me.'

She pulls her hood up and darts out into the daylight, using the statues as cover. With no time to think about it, Karim and I follow. As its December, there aren't any customers browsing the garden sculptures, so we cover a lot of ground quickly, weaving in and out of life-sized hippos and Roman pillars, trying not to knock anything over and start a domino chain of statues crashing into each other. It's a winding route, so difficult to know for sure, but I think we're heading for the far corner of the garden centre, furthest from the road where it borders the park.

We keep going, having to stop and hide from time to time when people – mostly people who work at Verge's – come into view, but we're making good progress. It isn't till we get to the climbing plants and fruit trees that I feel like something's changed. A group of about twenty people – some of them wearing the dark-green fleeces with the Verge's logo on it, and some of them looking like random customers – file down the paths that lead to the front of the garden centre and spread out, each taking a different aisle. It doesn't take a genius to work out that they're looking for something.

We're crouching half under and half in some massive prickly bush as we watch them making their way through the plants. They're being thorough – checking behind and under everything – which is bad because it means they'll find us if we stay here, but good because they're moving slowly. If we're quick, we can get away before they reach us.

Like she's read my mind, Kat backs out of the bush and scurries back down an aisle of trees, staying low and quiet. My mouth is as dry as my grandma's fruit cake, as I push Karim in front of me and we go after Kat. Every second I expect to hear a shout behind me, or feel a hand grabbing my ankle. Running while crouching over and fearing for your life is freaking exhausting and pretty much my whole body feels like it's on fire.

Out of the fruit trees and through a gate into a staff-only area, and Karim looks like he's about to drop. I've never been in this part of the garden centre before, but Kat seems to know where she's going. We circle around a toilet block and the industrial skip-like bins until we reach an enormous building with wood-panelled walls and a van-sized shuttered door at the front, which is sealed with a padlock as thick as my leg. Kat shoots past the door and around the side of the building. We just make it into the gap behind her when we hear what sounds like two sets of feet come marching up to the door. I shoot the others a warning look, and press back into the wall. I can't risk a look, but I can hear clearly enough.

The sound of metal clanking against metal rattles out of the quiet. They must be checking the door.

'It is secure,' he says. 'A human would be unable

to break this lock. We must resume our search elsewhere.'

'It is unlikely that the humans have left the site,' the second worker says, 'or the hive would have seen them.'

'Unlikely but not impossible. They had a head start, and there are many ways in and out of this place.'

'We are combing the aisles. We have eyes on all paths in the surrounding area. If they try to leave, they will be apprehended. If they are hiding, we will find them.'

A pause.

'We are at a critical stage. We cannot allow the humans to threaten the success of the second generation.'

'No human can defeat the hive.'

'I will patrol the perimeter.'

'I will return to stand guard.'

'At all costs.'

'At all costs.'

I try to steady my breathing as I listen to the crunch of their feet on the gravel path. That was too close. Then I count to one hundred before I start moving again, my mind replaying what we just overheard. *At all costs*. What does that mean?

The ground around the side of the building is compacted, icy mud. Moving across it is tricky. I try to keep my feet from flying out from under me, while the back of my coat keeps snagging on splinters in the wooden wall I'm leaning up against. By the time we make it to the back of the building, I'm just about done.

'I hope it's still here,' Kat whispers as she starts feeling around the wooden panels, gently pushing on each one.

'What are we looking for?' I say.

'One of these should slide,' she frowns. 'Aha!' The panel she's jiggling moves slightly. 'Give me a hand, it's supposed to be quite stiff.'

Kat pushes, and Karim and I pull, and after a bit of wiggling the panel slides across, leaving just enough space to crawl inside. Kat goes first, followed by Karim, and I get another great view of his butt as I go behind him. Once we're in, we pull the board back to hide the hole, but not quite all the way, so that we can get out quicker if we need to.

It's dim to the point of almost dark inside the

building, with just a small amount of light coming in through a couple of grimy windows. And all I can see are Christmas trees, looming up around us. There must be hundreds of them – all different sizes – their needled branches silhouetted in the gloom.

We find a hollow, just big enough for the three of us, where we can finally sit.

'This is nice,' Kat smiles, once we're huddled in together.

'Can't talk. Dying.' Karim leans his head back and closes his eyes.

'Have you got a snack, buddy?' I say. 'You should eat.'

Karim nods and pulls a cereal bar out of his pouch.

'First of all, I need to know how you found this place, Kat?' Even in the middle of trying not to be captured and spored by wasp people, the question had crossed my mind a couple of times.

'Eva worked here last Christmas,' Kat says. 'She's my older sister,' she adds for Karim's benefit. 'It's where they store the spare stock that they can't fit out on the display, so at Christmas it's full of trees to put out once the display ones have been sold. Eva used to sneak back here with her boyfriend so they could … be alone.' I can't see her face clearly, but I can hear the 'ew' in her voice.

'And she told you about it?' Karim says.

'No, she told her friend about it on the phone, and I happened to be listening. I didn't really want to – there was a lot of information that I would prefer never to have had enter my ears. But it was one of those car-crash moments; I couldn't tear myself away.'

'Good thing you didn't,' I say. 'This place is a life-saver.'

'So,' Kat says, as Karim chews on his bar. 'What next?'

And of course I've been thinking about this but my brain is a bit of a puddle, and it always helps to talk things through. 'We need to go through what we know, and what we don't,' I say. 'Then we can plan our next move.'

'OK, so we definitely have an alien situation. Somehow the spores have got into Straybridge and infected loads of people,' Kat says.

'Yes, loads of people, but not everyone,' I agree. 'I mean, we're all OK for some reason. The problem is we don't know how the spores have got in, or who is infected. Why some people and not others?'

'Until we know, it doesn't feel safe to go to sleep.'

'And until we know, we have to work on the basis that anyone could be a sporeling.'

Kat nods.

'The good news is,' I say, 'that they don't know we know. From what we overheard, they didn't ID us at the labs.'

'What was that creepy "*At all costs*" thing they said?' Karim asks through a mouthful. 'Is it their planet-invading catchphrase?'

'That's new,' I say. 'And we need to find out what it means.'

'So they're different from how they were at Crater Lake?'

'There are quite a few differences,' Kat says. 'At Crater Lake you could tell they were bugs from looking at their eyes; but the eyes on the new sporelings seem normal.'

'And there were two types before: workers and hunters. Workers weren't really a threat unless you attacked them, they just got on with the jobs they were supposed to do. Hunters were smart and fast and in charge. And they really wanted to hurt-slash-infect us.'

'None of the ones we saw today seemed workery,' Kat says. 'They're more switched on. Also, it isn't obvious what jobs they're doing. At Crater Lake they were always busy building the dam and draining the lake.'

'They must be working on jobs we don't know about yet. And both Karim's mum and my mum have tried to fool us into doing what they want,' I say. 'There's a level of cunning there that makes them much more dangerous.'

'So you think they're basically all hunters?' Karim says.

'Or something between workers and hunters. They're definitely nastier than workers.'

'Great,' Karim sighs.

'There's something that's bothering me,' I say. 'And I feel like it's key to whatever's going on here. Remember all those weirdos staring at us when we were walking through town?'

Karim and Kat nod.

'And it was interesting how someone came into the tunnel as soon as your mum was awake and knew someone was outside her door, Karim. I don't think it was a coincidence.' And, as I'm saying it, I get more and more sure. 'I think they are communicating somehow.'

'But there are no phones or internet,' Karim says. 'So how?'

'I reckon they have some kind of link – I'm not Ade so I don't know how it would work exactly – but I'm sure they know what each other is seeing and thinking.'

'Ooh, like a hive mind?' Kat's eyes widen. 'That's gonna make things tricky.'

'So tricky,' I say. 'What one of them knows, all of them know.'

'So if one of them spots us, they all know where we are?' Karim says.

'I reckon so,' I say.

We all sit in silence for a moment and I'm sure that, like me, Kat and Karim are trying to get their heads around how impossible our situation seems. I wish Chets, Mak and Ade were with us, but I don't know if they've been spored or if they'd help us even if they are still human. Things went so bad with Ade and Mak.

'Lance?' Karim says. 'What do we do?'

'We face this one challenge at a time,' I say, getting my focus back where it needs to be. 'So we get away from here without being seen, and we try to find out how the spores got into Straybridge. We can't get rid of them if we don't know where they're coming from.'

'But where do we start?' Kat says.

'There's definitely not a meteor hole, right?' Karim is starting to look a bit better, now that he's eaten, but I know he needs a proper rest.

'I'm not sure,' I say, and it's frustrating as hell because I wish I could come up with all the answers. 'But we need to regroup – we can't fight and win if we can barely move.'

'So your plan is to get some sleep? Isn't that the exact opposite of a good thing to do in this situation?' Karim says. 'Won't we turn into those things?'

'We've all been sleeping in Straybridge, in our houses, and none of us have turned. I have my CPAP at home, so I'll be safe. Karim, we know your house is clean because your mum only turned when she was locked in the lab. And Kat, your house seemed fine, too. I think animals can sense the spores, and Nugget was acting like his usual self.'

'But your mum, Lance,' Kat says. 'You shouldn't be around her.'

'If I don't go home, she'll know something's up. If I go home and act normal, the hive won't suspect we're planning anything and we'll keep that advantage. I can shut myself in my room. And if your mum comes home, Karim, just avoid her as much as possible. She won't openly attack you – she'll be pretending she's still human.'

'I'm not feeling good about this plan, Lance,' Karim says.

'But if you don't get proper rest and food, you're done for anyway,' I say. I see Kat shoot me a quick look, but she covers it. 'And it's just for one night. Tomorrow we sort this town out.'

'But first we have to make it back without being seen,' Kat says.

'We'll wait for the curfew bells, then sneak out the back, cut through the park and graveyard and then follow the river back up to Karim's estate. There are hardly any houses that way, so we have a good chance of getting all the way to town unnoticed.'

Kat grins at me. 'We got this.'

'We so do.'

'You two are bat-poo crazy,' Karim says. 'And I'm only doing your plan because I'm the noob and I don't know my way around town. And I'm not happy about all the jogging that lies ahead.'

'Rest up,' I say. 'Have another cereal bar.'

'I'm just gonna lay back a while,' Karim nestles back against the trunk of one of the larger trees. 'Don't worry, I'll keep my eyes open. Do you think there's anywhere we can get some water? My mouth is so dry I can hardly swallow.'

'I think we could risk having a look around in here for something. The door's locked and we'll be able to hear if someone unlocks it.' I'm dead thirsty too, and wishing I had a backpack of supplies like at Crater Lake. 'You guys stay here and stay alert. I'll be back in a few minutes.' I almost add a 'please look after Karim, Kat' but think better of it. She'll look after him without me asking anyway.

I wiggle out of our hollow and skulk through the trees, enjoying being able to walk without crouching down. Most of the trees in here are way taller than I am. As I snake through the Christmas trees, making sure to remember the route I take, I notice that all the trees in here are the new pines like we have at home, with those perfectly spherical cones tightly curled up. They're all planted upright in pots rather than being cut and leaning, so it really is like taking a stroll through a mountain forest. Well, not exactly like that cos I'm in a giant warehouse, but you know what I mean. They rear up in the dim light, branches like fingers catching on my clothes and in my hair, and unfamiliar shapes seem to form in the shadows. It would be sinister if I hadn't already seen way creepier things today.

When I get close to the front of the building, the trees start to thin out and I see that there's a desk in the corner covered in paperwork, with a couple of chairs and some boxes stacked up beside it. I stand for a moment, straining my ears for any signs of movement at the front door, and then I break cover, darting over to the desk. I use the soft glow from the lock screen on my phone to help me look through the desk drawers and the boxes. It feels reassuring to have my phone in my hand again, even if the only thing it's good for right now is being used as a torch. After a rummage, I hit the jackpot – two unopened bottles of water, a slightly bruised apple and half a box of Lindor balls. I zip the chocolate and water into my coat pockets, and on second thoughts put the apple back with a £2 coin so I don't completely feel like I'm stealing. Then I head back into the trees, my phone still in my hand.

I'm most of the way back, and way too excited about showing the others my stash, when I spot a movement out of the corner of my eye, and my heart almost leaps out of my chest. I jump backwards, knocking into a tree which wobbles in one of those butt-clenching slow-mo moments where you see your life flash before your eyes. I grapple with a couple of branches and just manage to stop it from crashing down, cursing myself for being so damn jumpy. Once I've quadruple checked that it's back on its feet and not going anywhere, I return my attention to what caused my almost accident which I'm assuming at this point is not something that's going to jump out and attack me, cos let's face it, it would have already done that by now.

I swing my phone slowly and carefully back and forth around where that whatever-it-was caught my eye, and it doesn't take long for me to see it: the glint of something shiny, tucked, half hidden, in the roots of a huge tree. So of course I think someone must have dropped something down there, and I use my hands to dig it out.

It takes me a moment to work out what it is. It's dirty and torn and obviously the light's not great. And then it clicks into place, and my mind is racing at a million miles a second. I pelt back to Kat and Karim and skid into the hollow.

'What is it?' Kat says. 'Is someone coming?'

I shake my head and hold out the tiny shiny thing that's changed everything. She takes it and peers at it. Karim sits up and leans over it, too.

'Isn't that a WWE card?' he says. 'Am I totally missing something here?'

'It's a limited-edition John Cena WWE wrestling card,' I say.

'Oh,' Kat says. 'Jordan at Montmorency had one of these, do you remember? He was so sad when he lost it...'

'At Crater Lake,' I finish for her.

'Where did you find it?' Karim asks.

'It was in the trees,' I say. 'Guys: it's the trees.'

10
The Bells

It makes sense when we think it through. The slopes of the crater were covered in woodland, and I remember there being loads of pine trees.

'So, they were growing in the crater and were surrounded by spores,' I say. 'Is it possible the trees absorbed them somehow?'

'The aliens had lots of similarities with parasitic wasps. I'm sure I've seen somewhere that some wasps use trees to implant their larvae and it does abnormal stuff to the trees.' Kat takes a sip of water.

'Yes,' I say, remembering how we all tried to learn loads about wasps when we got back from Crater Lake, just in case. 'I can't remember what they were called, but there were some pictures of deformed acorns that looked like exploding brains.'

'So the trees could be releasing the spores,'

Karim gasps. 'I have one in my house, guys. This is so bad.'

'That's right, you do,' I say. 'But you've not gone buggy.'

'Is your tree one of these, Lance?' Kat asks.

'Yeah,' I say. 'A big one.'

'Maybe Karim's is too small,' says Kat.

'Or maybe I'm immune – it could be my secondary superpower.'

'Or maybe I've got this completely wrong. There's more than one John Cena card in the world.' I feel so frustrated. I need to know for sure.

'But it is limited edition,' says Kat. 'There aren't that many. I think you're right, I really do. We're just still missing something.'

'And in the meantime, we're stuck in a shed, surrounded by evil body-snatcher trees.' Karim chucks a Lindor in his mouth. 'So yeah, everything's cool.'

'If it is the trees,' I say, 'I can't believe they came to Straybridge by accident. Someone has planned this.'

'Oh great, an evil mastermind,' Karim says. 'Now it's a party.'

I can't help but laugh, at the same time Kat does.

'How is this funny?' Karim says. 'It's literally the end of the world.'

'Not if we stop it,' I say.

'Three kids against a whole town?' Karim says.

I gulp down some water. It's like the nicest drink I've had in my entire life. 'Tomorrow we'll get some back-up.'

Karim raises an eyebrow. 'And by back-up, I'm hoping you mean the army, Tony Stark and Godzilla.'

'Even better,' I smile.

We try to chill out and rest while we can, although it's pretty hard now that we know there are probably millions of alien spores floating all around us, along with a pack of hostile sporelings just outside in the garden centre. Our hiding place slowly grows darker around us as the sun starts to set, and we're more than ready to make an exit by the time the first chimes ring.

We leave the stock shed of horror the same way we came in, sneaking around the side of the building in the failing light and out of the staff-only area, back into the main garden centre. We have our hoods up and scarves tied around our mouths and noses, so the only parts of our faces that are visible are our eyes. Any customers are on their way home in time for curfew, so the aisles are dark and empty and the only sound I can hear is the jangling of keys, as somebody locks up the café. We've decided to try to get out of the back gates before they're locked for the night, assuming the coast is clear, so we head that way, using the display Christmas trees for cover, and hoping we won't have to resort to our back-up plan, which involves crossing more of the centre, and is even riskier.

We lurk in the trees, close to the gate, waiting for the perfect moment to sneak out. Though of course there never is a perfect moment for anything really – you just have to make your choice and go with it, and try as hard as you can to not mess it up. The sound of a large vehicle coming up the road makes me hold back a moment, and we watch as a delivery truck turns into the gate, loaded with more Christmas trees. The driver pulls up, opens the door and climbs down from the cab with a clipboard, leaving the door open.

'I know a way we can find out for sure where those trees have come from,' Karim says, stepping out into the open.

Before I can even get my head around what he's doing, he runs to the truck and climbs into the cab.

'He's not going to try to drive that truck, is he?' Kat squeaks through her scarf.

'I honestly don't know,' I say, starting after him.

By the time I get to the cab, Karim is already jumping back out. 'We'd better run,' he says, darting towards the gates.

'Hey!' I hear a shout behind me, and the crunch of footsteps on gravel. 'Stop right there!'

Of course, that makes us move faster. The gates are just ahead and open wide – we only have to get there. And then they start to close.

'Oh man,' I say. 'They must be operating them from the office.' We're not going to make it. 'Plan B – back into the trees!'

We turn sharply, and speed into the Christmas trees, smashing through the branches and plummeting into darkness. I hear shouts and heavy footsteps following me, and I lose track of Karim and Kat. I turn my head from side to side, trying to catch a glimpse of them, but all I see are shadows. Shadows, and branches that pull at my clothes and scratch at my face. An arm jerks towards me from between two trees on my right, clutching at my sleeve and holding tight. I pull away as hard as I can, but the hand feels superglued to my arm. So I kick out with everything I've got, making contact with something that I hope is a leg and not a tree trunk. I hear a grunt, and the hand tears away from my coat with a ripping sound, so I run again, crashing through the trees. A person-shaped shadow looms out of the murk in front of me, so I make a sharp turn to the left, while at the same time shoving a ceiling-high tree towards it.

At the side of Verge's garden centre there's a separate building that sells pond stuff – weed and rocks and loads of different fish. I used to visit it for a Sunday treat when I was younger, spending ages watching the koi shimmer around their pool. It has a small exit that leads straight into the car park. Now it's our only option.

I turn the opposite way. If they know we're making for Verge Aquatics, they'll have people waiting there for us for sure. It has to be unexpected. I make like I'm heading towards the front entrance, running like the floor is actual lava, and it's only when I break out of the trees that I leg it back to Aquatics and battering-ram the door, which luckily opens easily because I'm not the biggest guy and if it was me versus a solid door, I reckon my chances of coming out on top are slim.

'What took you so long?' Kat beams at me from just inside the door. Karim, next to her, looks like he's just run through a forest of Christmas trees away from an evil alien swarm. They push a shelving unit in front of the door, cos apparently blocking doors after we've gone through them is our new thing, and then we charge through the store to the exit, out into the car park and away.

We have a tiny head start, and we have to use it to disappear. We jump the low fence into the park and run through it like we're being chased by the actual Demogorgon. The park leads to the graveyard, which is quiet and still, the moonlight glinting off the marble headstones in a way that I might have found creepy if I wasn't running for my life. My lungs feel ready to burst as we tear down the path, startling a lonely fox out doing whatever foxes do when we're all inside.

'Sorry!' Kat says to it, as we speed past.

I'm relieved to finally see the big road bridge up

ahead. We half fall down the steep verge, which is icy hard, and once we're hidden underneath, surrounded by the graffitied concrete, we allow ourselves a minute of rest. We squat in the shadows, our backs against a pillar that stinks of pee, all of us trying to catch our breath. I risk pulling the scarf down from my nose and mouth, so that I can enjoy the feeling of the freezing air being sucked into my lungs. I know we need to get moving quickly, but we're going to be much harder to find if we're not all rasping like we've just done a whole lesson of circuit training which is, no question, the absolute worst type of PE that they force you to do at high school.

It takes maybe two minutes for us to recover enough to stand up and talk, which isn't that long considering how hard we pushed ourselves. Must be all that circuit training.

'How did you know about this place?' Karim asks, looking around at the adult graffiti and burnt-up ground covered in empty beer cans. 'Are you in a gang you haven't told me about? Because, if so, I'd like to join. I was made for the gangster life.'

Kat and I both laugh. When you skateboard in places you're not supposed to, you sometimes get chased by security guards, and it was on one of those occasions that we found this spot under the bridge. It's totally grim, but unless you knew it was there, or you found it by accident when you were running away from a big bald guy threatening to call your mum, you'd never spot it.

'It's come in handy once or twice,' I say. 'And what the hell were you doing inside that truck?'

'Ooh, tell him, Karim,' Kat says. 'It's so clever.'

'I was checking the sat nav,' Karim says, not even trying not to look smug. 'So we would know for sure where the trees came from.'

'That is actually genius,' I say. 'And?'

'I'll give you one guess,' Karim says.

'Is it wrong that part of me feels relieved?' I say. 'Assuming that you are actually talking about Crater Lake and not Norway or something.'

'Very wrong,' Karim says. 'You strange, twisted person.'

'But we know what we're dealing with now. We can work out how to fix it.'

'Yeah, I'd still rather the trees had come from Norway,' Karim says.

I'm aware that time is ticking and we're not out of danger yet.

'Come on, we need to keep going. If we stay as close as we can to the verge, we'll be hidden by the overhang, so we should be hard to see. It's not the quickest way back, but I think it's our best option.'

So we press our backs to the sort-of cliff face of land that separates the river from the main part of Straybridge. In the summer it's covered in shrubs and wild flowers, but at this time of year, it's mostly bald earth, embedded with rocks that dig into our backs as we side-step along. If we slip, we'll go straight into the river, which I know from experience is even colder than the worst cold you could imagine. It's slow going, and we're concentrating too hard on stopping our feet slipping out from under us to talk. There are no signs of human life. I've never known Straybridge this quiet.

The river runs through the golf course and cricket ground, which are, from what we can see, completely empty of people right now. The wind buffets the trees, making branches creak and groan, and the river flows in front of us: sparkling ripples fluttering over black depths. I hear a faint drip, drip, drip as the water trickles into a storm drain. I imagine the air would smell of frost and earth, but all I can smell is the inside of my scarf, which I can't remember having put in the wash, like, ever, so I'm not gonna lie, it isn't exactly fresh. But who washes their scarf? I find myself wondering what Kat's scarf smells like, and I reckon it's white chocolate muffins, or buttery popcorn.

And then a sound hits my ears that is totally out of place. It's a sort of thrumming – a vibration in the air above us. I freeze and press back into the verge, putting my hand out to push Kat and Karim back with me. I don't need to – they've heard it too.

The noise is growing steadily louder and it's just so weirdly out of place that I know it can't be good. We huddle together and as far back into the ground behind us as we can – trying to make ourselves invisible. I don't think any of us are breathing.

It's a steady sound. Constant. No ups and downs or stops and starts. Just a low buzz, getting closer. Of course I look up, trying to see whatever it is that I can hear. But we're under an overhang and all I can see is packed mud and a few dangling roots from the plants above. The sky on the other side of the river is clear. Whatever is moving toward us is coming from behind.

Every millimetre of my skin is hypersensitive, feeling each tiny movement in the air, every brush of my clothes against my body, all of the places where the rocky verge is pressed into my back. I can feel Kat shaking next to me, and I squeeze her hand. To be honest, it's as much for me as it is for her. The buzzing moves closer and, though the logical part of my brain has decided it's most likely a drone of some kind, I know in my heart that it's something much worse.

As the thrumming fills my ears, I see a change in the river in front of us. The swirling ripples are flattened away as the surface becomes eggshell smooth, and then it vibrates violently in raised lines and parallel troughs. It moves like the mesh covering on your headphones when you're playing music really loud. Whatever this thing is, it's right above us, and it's big. The louder it gets, the more we try to disappear into the dirt behind us. My mind picks through our options, though as we have no idea what we're dealing with, everything is based on guesses and hope. If it comes to it, we'll have to break cover and run, but assuming this thing is fast, and that it's part of the hive, that has to be a last resort.

It doesn't know we're here, I tell myself. It has loads of ground to cover, and it can't know the town like we do. It doesn't know about the overhang, and it will only search this area for so long before it moves on. Once again, our best bet is to do nothing. So we sit tight. Hold our nerve.

For a moment, the sky above us seems to grow a little darker, like a cloud has blown across the moon. The river throbs. There is no sound except for the buzz. I brace myself to run, trying to work out where I could get a weapon. A tree branch might work, or a spade or something with a long handle. There must be a groundsman's shed here somewhere.

But then the shadow passes, the river calms, and the god-awful buzz starts to move away. We wait as the sound lessens, whirring away to nothing. And then we wait some more.

'Seeing as you two know way more about this stuff than I do,' Karim says, his voice scratchy, 'I would love for you to tell me what the hell that was.'

11
Hunter

'I honestly don't know for sure,' I say.

'Then hit me with your best guess.'

I don't know whether to tell him what I'm thinking. I mean, it's nuts, and it's also terrifying. But he's come this far with us and he hasn't totally lost it yet, so I figure I owe him honesty.

'Back at Crater Lake,' I say, 'we only saw one of the sporelings fully transform.'

'Digger.' Kat shudders.

'Kat trapped him on the climbing wall. He was still superglued there when the police and our parents arrived.'

'And what does the final evolution of an alien sporeling look like?' Karim says.

'Huge,' Kat says. 'Matte-black furry bits. Bulgy eyes.'

'I remember there being some goo involved,' I add. 'And that its head looked like a mouldy potato.'

'And,' Kat says. She's still holding my hand. 'It had wings.'

'Cool, cool, cool,' Karim says. 'And do you know what happened to this Digger-slash-flying-alien-creature?'

Neither of us say anything. After Crater Lake we were all spoken to by shady government people, who did their best to convince us that what happened at the activity centre was a hallucination as a result of heat exhaustion, mixed with the toxic fumes from a bad batch of paint used on the walls in the dorms. We were told not to talk about it. They didn't go as far as threatening us, but the warning was there, hanging in the air between us. The only answers we got were clearly total bull, so we stopped asking.

'Right,' says Karim. 'So what you're saying is that the escaped creature they told us about probably isn't a bunny.'

'That's something that's been bothering me,' I say. 'There was no structural damage inside the labs. No sign of smoke damage, or broken doors, no evidence of anything escaping.'

'So you're saying you don't think Digger, if it is Digger, escaped,' Kat says.

I nod. 'I think he was released.'

'On purpose?' Karim says.

'Yeah. Maybe as a cover for whatever's going on in Straybridge. Maybe to do something that we don't know about yet.' I close my eyes for a moment, realising how tired I am, as the curfew bells ring out across the town. 'We should get going – we're gonna have some explaining to do when we get back, and we all need to rest.'

'I don't think I'll ever sleep again,' Karim says, as we go back to side-stepping up the river.

It takes us around twenty minutes to get through the rest of the golf course and cricket grounds, and then we pass the closed and dark Straybridge Community Hall, until we finally reach the border of Karim's estate. There's no way we can get through the estate without being seen, so we take down our hoods, stuff our scarves in our pockets and put our cover story into action.

'Karim, look as sick as you can,' I say.

'Won't be hard, I feel like poo,' he nods. And even though he says it with a smile, I can see that he's struggling.

Kat and I walk either side of him, our arms around him to support him. Then we walk quickly through the streets, trying to look like we're walking quickly cos Karim is ill and we're out past curfew, rather than because we just snuck into a secret lab, got chased through a forest of Christmas trees, and almost got found and potentially ripped apart by an unidentified flying object that might have been the alien wasp formerly known as Digger.

There's no one on the roads, but the houses all have their lights on and we see a few twitching curtains as we pass. When we get to Karim's, he doesn't even have a chance to get his key in the door before his dad has opened it and is standing there looking mad as hell.

'Where have you been? I've been worried sick.'

'I'm sorry, Dad. We were at Kat's house, and...'

'Who is Kat? I've never heard of this Kat before?' Karim's dad says, so angry that even his beard looks full of rage.

'I'm Katja, Mr Amrani,' Kat says, in that way she has of making even the most basic words sound like music. 'I'm sorry we haven't met before – I know Karim from school.'

Karim's dad looks at her and you can literally see his beard calm down.

'It's nice to meet you, Katja,' he says.

'We went to the park to have a walk before the curfew bells, and I realised I'd forgotten to eat.' Karim puts on a genuinely impressive, sad-puppy face.

'Karim, you know you have to take responsibility for yourself,' Karim's dad says, but he's more worried than mad now. 'Come inside, let's sort you out.'

Karim puts one foot in the door and hesitates. 'Is Mum home yet?'

'Not yet, but she said she'd be very late. She has so much to sort out.' He ruffles Karim's hair. 'And you've still got me to look after you.' He looks at me and Kat. 'Would you like to come in for some dinner?'

I so want to go in for some dinner. 'Thanks, but we'd better get home. My mum will be worried,' I say.

'Mine too,' says Kat. 'But I hope to see you again soon.'

'OK, no problem. But I should run you back,' he says. 'I can't let you walk home alone.'

And though I'd love to walk back with Kat so we can talk, it will actually help our story if I arrive home with Karim's dad to back me up.

'OK, thanks,' I say. 'That would be great.'

'Give me two minutes,' he says, helping Karim inside. I hear him saying what a nice girl Kat seems, in between telling Karim off for not taking care of himself properly. Kat gives me a grin. She looks dead tired, and I hope she can get some sleep tonight. I also hope that getting some sleep doesn't mean I lose her to the hive.

'I'll be ready to leave at first bells,' she whispers, like she's read my mind, and I know that whatever tomorrow holds, having her with me is going to make it a whole lot more bearable.

'Right, let's get you two back.' Karim's dad comes out, jingling his car keys. 'Can't have you running around Straybridge with a potentially dangerous creature on the loose.'

We drop Kat off first, and she gives my hand one last squeeze before she gets out of the car. Karim's dad goes with her to her front door and has a quick chat to her mum, and then we're driving up the road to my house.

I feel sick as we get out of the car, and even sicker as we cross the drive. I want to run. Back to Kat's or Karim's, or anywhere really. I could tell Mum I'm grabbing my portable CPAP and going for a sleepover. But she'd suspect, I know she would.

She opens the front door before Karim's dad has even taken his finger from the bell button, and stands there like the villain in a horror movie, silhouetted against the light, and with heat blasting out from behind her.

'Hi Lorna,' Karim's dad says. 'I thought you might like this one bringing back,' he smiles and puts his hand on my shoulder.

'Thank you, I was getting very worried,' she says, slowly and carefully, like it's a speech she's been practising. 'Where on earth have you been, Lance?'

'He and Karim were at Katja's house, and then they all went for a walk. Unfortunately, Karim forgot to eat, and became unwell, so Lance and Katja helped him home.'

'I'm sorry to hear that Karim is ill,' Mum says. 'There's nothing worse than having a body that fails you.'

There really is, Mum, I think, looking at the stranger in front of me. My actual mum always says that she's proud of how her body keeps going, even though some parts of it don't work properly.

'He's eating and resting at home, so he'll feel better soon. I'm very grateful to your Lance for taking care of him.' Karim's dad smiles.

'Lance is always trying to be a hero.' Mum looks at me through cold eyes.

'I expect he needs some food and rest, too,' Karim's dad says. 'I'd better get back to Karim. Nadia's still at work, and I'd rather not leave him alone for too long.'

'Of course she is – she has lots to do, I'm sure.'

They're probably communicating right now. I wish I could know what they're saying.

'Thanks for the lift,' I say, stepping into the freaking ridiculously hot house.

'You're welcome, Lance. See you soon. Take care, Lorna.'

And then he's gone, and it's just me and the thing that used to be my mum.

12
Playing the Game

'Come through to the kitchen when you've taken your coat off,' Mum says. 'You need to eat.'

I break the record for the slowest-ever removal of coat and shoes, and walk through to the kitchen where Mum is standing over a big pan on the cooker, slowly stirring with a wooden spoon.

'You didn't need to cook for me, Mum,' I say. 'I can just grab something from the fridge.'

'It's no trouble,' she says. 'You've had a busy day – you need something nutritious. Why don't you sit down at the table?'

I pull out one of the heavy kitchen chairs, gritting my teeth as it makes an awful scraping sound on the floor. Mum hates it when I do that. But then I think, hey, at least I'm acting normal. It's harder than you might think when your mum has been body-snatched by parasitic alien wasps.

I sit down at the table, and for a moment there

is just the scrape of the spoon against the inside of the pan, and a bubbling from whatever's inside.

'Where did you go for your walk today?' she says, not turning her head from the pan.

'We went to the park this afternoon, just for a bit before the curfew bells,' I say.

'The park and Katja's house.' She turns off the heat on the cooker. 'Nowhere else?'

She knows we were at the university this morning. Of course she does – half the hive saw us. I choose my words carefully and try to sound as casual as possible.

'We went with Karim to the university earlier – he wanted to see his mum, and cos the phones aren't working, he made us trek all the way to her office.'

'And did you see her?' Mum is getting a bowl out of the cupboard.

'No, they have security people there, and they wouldn't let him in. Then my old teacher turned up and apparently forgot she isn't my teacher anymore.'

'Your teacher?' She opens the drawer and takes out a spoon.

'Miss Hoche. The one who thinks she's Lois

Lane or something now. She said some things that hacked me off, so we left and went back to Kat's.'

Mum pours the contents of the pan into the bowl, the steam puffing up and clouding over her face. Then she brings the bowl to the table and puts it in front of me. Tomato soup.

'Eat up,' she says, tilting her head again in that way that makes spiders scuttle down my back.

I look at the soup and swallow down the bit of sick that gushes into my mouth. I haven't eaten soup since before the summer. And I can't eat this. What if she put a sedative in it, like Digger did at Crater Lake? What if I fall asleep at the table?

'It was your favourite when you were little,' she says. She's testing me.

'I know it was,' I say. 'But I went off it after Crater Lake, remember?'

'Isn't it time you got over that?' she says. 'It was six months ago, and a lot has changed since then.'

I look at her. Try to keep my face neutral. Every one of her words has a weight to it. They're so heavy with suspicion and threat that I'm surprised they don't thud onto the table and knock over my soup. What I say next matters so much.

'I hear you, Mum, but it's really hard. How do you get over something like that?'

She smiles at me. 'You adapt and grow. Nobody ever made a success of their life by staying the same.'

I smile back, with as much warmth as I can. 'You're quite clever for an old person,' I say, cos that's something I call her when we're mucking around and I'm being cheeky. 'And I know you're right. I'll try harder, I promise.'

Her smile widens, and I look into her eyes, like *really* look, to see if I can see any of the real mum in there. If I can find her, maybe I can get her to fight the parasite that's controlling her body. That happens in movies sometimes – the humanity wins out because love conquers all and all that shiz. We've all seen it. But this ain't a movie, and all I see in my mum's eyes is a chilling look of satisfaction that she thinks she's won me over. So I guess we're going to have to do this the horrifying, drawn-out way. And first things first, how the hell am I going to avoid eating this soup?

So, options are to drop it, which is blatantly obvious, to ruin it somehow, which is totally obvious, or to distract her and get rid of it, which is also massively obvious. I settle for stirring it while I try to decide what to do.

'How was your day, Mum?' I ask, which is normal because I always ask. 'I'm just gonna get some bread to dunk in my soup.' I push my chair back, leave the bowl on the table, and go over to the kitchen counter.

'Frustrating,' she says. 'There are so many things that need to be done, but the time's not right.'

I bend down to get a plate out of the cupboard. 'You mean because you're still not feeling well enough?'

'I feel well,' she says, 'but I'm limited by other things.'

'Like what?' I take the clip off the bread and take out four slices. 'Anything I can help with?'

I hear her sigh behind me. 'You can certainly help me at some point, but you're not ready yet.'

I let out a snort of laughter as I put the clip back on the bread bag and head to the fridge. 'You sound like my Jedi master.'

'Hmm, I think we are a little like the Jedi. They serve the greater good of their people, sacrificing everything for duty.'

I wonder if she means that she had to sacrifice her happiness to have me, and that stings. But I'm pretty sure that when she says 'we', she doesn't mean her and me, and I'm annoyed that she's desecrating something as sacred as the Jedi order with her creepy-bug mentality.

'I hope the Jedi Council doesn't expect me to give up bread with my soup, cos that's one sacrifice too far.' I open the fridge.

'The Jedi have a council?'

'Of course, Mum,' I say. 'So they can make group decisions. So they're fair.'

'Ha,' she snorts. 'That's their weakness, then. They'd be more powerful if they had just one master – someone to make all the rules and to protect at all costs.'

'Like Emperor Palpatine?' I peer around the fridge at her. 'The evil Sith Lord? Yeah, that worked out well.' Good to get more confirmation of what side she's on.

'Hurry up and close that, it's freezing in here,' she says.

I take the spread out and close the fridge. 'Seriously, though, Mum, if you need more help around the house, you just have to say.'

'They're more outside-of-the-house jobs,' she says. 'And you've done so much for me over the years, the most important thing you can do now is take care of yourself. Eat and rest.'

I try not to shudder as I butter the bread, nice and thick cos I like a high butter to anything ratio. 'Actually,' I say, 'being out after curfew has made me a bit uneasy. Have you checked the house for any signs of the escaped test creature from the lab?'

'I can assure you that the creature from the lab is not inside this house.'

I put the spread back in the fridge. I'm running out of time and ideas. 'I know it's pathetic,' I say. 'But would you mind checking again for me? It would help me to sleep better tonight.'

'Sit down and eat your soup,' she says. 'And then we'll check together so you can see for yourself that the only living things in this house are me and you.'

I put my plate of buttered bread down on the table and lower myself back into my chair. She watches as I pick up the spoon and sink it into the bowl.

'I made it myself, you know,' she says, and I try not to immediately chuck the bowl across the kitchen in horror. The sweet smell of tomatoes wafts up my nose and I have to focus on not gagging. Mum just watches as I lift a spoonful up to my mouth and touch it to my lips.

'Oh man,' I say. 'It's gone cold. I'm just gonna warm it in the microwave.'

Obvious or not, I have to get rid of this soup. I'm either going to blow it up in the microwave or make it so hot that I drop the bowl. I can't eat it.

I pick up the bowl and carefully carry it over to the counter, saying, 'You know I think your hair *is* shinier, Mum.' She only gets up off her seat and comes with me, watching as I open the microwave door and put the bowl inside.

'You've left the spoon in, Lance.' Mum reaches in and takes it. 'No metal in the microwave, remember, you might blow up the house.'

'Oh god, I'm such an idiot.' That's plan A out the window. 'Sorry, Mum, it's been a mental day.'

'It's OK, my love, it will all feel better after food and sleep.'

I close the microwave door, set the power to full, and hit the start button. Mum always says I should set the timer, but I like living on the edge and just seeing how it goes.

As the microwave whirrs, the bowl beginning to spin slowly inside, I wonder whether I'm going to have to just make a run for it. I could go to Kat's. It's only a few minutes down the road – I might be able to make it. But the bug-eyes at Crater Lake were all strong and fast, and I don't know what my mum is capable of, physically. She might be on me before I reach the front door. Or I could hit her over the head with the bowl, but I know I won't be able to bring myself to do that. There might be an alien inside, but it's still my mum's body. I can't hurt her. So, dropping the soup it is. It's obvious, but I'll have to make a big show of being gutted and hope she buys it.

Something splatters onto my foot. I look down to see a blob of red liquid soaking into my sock, and I think for a moment that I must be bleeding. But then I turn to look at Mum and I see that the red splatter is coming from the spoon she's still holding. Tomato soup is dripping onto the floor.

'Mum,' I say. 'You're getting soup everywhere.'

She doesn't answer. Doesn't move. Just stands there, frozen, holding the dripping spoon, staring at the bowl in the microwave turning in the yellow light.

'Mum?' I wave my hand in front of her face but she doesn't even blink. She's glitching again, like she did when she turned weird. For half a second, I allow myself to hope that maybe she's gonna turn back to normal again. Maybe the process is reversing. But what if it's not. This is my chance to act, and I can't waste it cos I'm having some childish fairy-tale fantasy that clearly isn't going to come true because we all know life's not like that.

I pause the microwave to take out the soup, thinking I can trash it while Mum's in glitch mode. I keep my eyes on her the whole time. Last time it happened, she was glitched for at least a few minutes, but this time, only one or two seconds after the bowl stops turning, she blinks and her eyes flick to my face.

I panic, and my finger hits the restart button on the microwave. The moment it hums into action, her expression goes blank, like the light's been switched off in her brain. It must be the microwave. I don't know how or why it's putting her out of action, but right now I don't care. This is a freaking breakthrough. This is something I can use.

But how can I use it? Will it only glitch her for a certain amount of time? Or will she keep glitching as long as it's on? I'm a bit worried that it might actually damage her if I leave it going for too long. I mean it's clearly doing something to her brain, right? And then there are the others. If all of the sporelings are connected, they're going to know that something is up with her. They might swarm over here and get all aggressive, like they did at Crater Lake. If you attacked one, the others went nuts. I know they're different this time, but it's still worth being cautious. I need time to think about this. I need to talk to the others.

For now I focus on the immediate problem: the soup. The trouble is, if I turn off the microwave to get rid of the soup, Mum will unglitch and see me. So I need to think outside the box. The digital clock on the microwave counts the seconds I spend being unable to come up with a plan, and I honestly couldn't feel more stressed if it was the timer on a bomb, ticking down to my death.

A soft bump behind me makes me turn to see Betty running into the kitchen to her food bowl. She looks up at me and Mum but doesn't go psycho like she did last night, so I'm thinking that maybe when Mum is glitched, she doesn't freak out cats in the same way. And that gives me an idea. You know in superhero movies when there's a character with super speed, and they run around too fast for anyone to see, setting up the room so that stuff falls on people and the bad guys punch each other instead of the heroes? Sometimes they do it with characters who can stop time, too. It was awesome the first time I saw it, but it's been so overdone now. Anyway, I reckon if I can set things up just right, I might be able to get away with destroying the evil soup. So, I get a couple of Betty's favourite treats from the tin, then call her over and up onto the counter top. I have to get the timing perfect and I'm sweating like a pig up a tree. I count myself down from three, but go on two, just to jumpstart myself into getting it done.

In one swift movement, I put a treat on the counter, right in front of Mum, turn off the microwave, open the door, and pick up the hot bowl with a tea towel. As Mum unglitches, I make sure my arm is right next to Betty. She suddenly goes nuts, arching her back and screeching. She leaps off the counter, knocking my arm so that the bowl of soup goes flying out of my hand and smashes on the floor.

'Oh man!' I say, as Betty darts out of the cat flap. I feel a bit bad and make a silent promise to give her extra treats when this is all over.

'Foolish cat,' Mum yells, as the two pieces of bowl roll on the tiles, and the puddle of soup pools around our feet.

I jump out of the soup lava, and start trying to clean it with the tea towel. 'I'm so sorry, Mum,' I say. 'I dunno what's wrong with her. She seemed fine and then she just lost it out of the blue.'

Mum gets the kitchen roll and starts cleaning, too. She doesn't say anything, but I can almost see rage seething out of her.

'Mum?' I say. 'Are you alright? I'm really sorry about the soup.' I know it's a lie, but I'm pretty sure that lying is acceptable in this situation.

She takes a breath. 'It wasn't your fault,' she says. 'But I will have to do something about that cat.'

Oh shiz. RIP Betty. At least she's a fast runner. 'I'm actually really tired,' I say. 'Can I take my bread upstairs and watch TV in bed, please?'

She stops mopping at that, looks up and smiles.

'Of course, sweetheart. Go and get comfortable, and don't stay up too late. I'll finish cleaning up.'

'You're the best,' I say. I grab the bread, some crisps, a banana, a pack of cookies and a drink, and walk as calmly as I can out of the kitchen.

'Lance?' Mum calls me.

I bite my lip. Stop. Look back. 'Yes, Mum?'

'Sweet dreams,' she smiles.

I force myself to smile back, then make my way upstairs to the safety of my room. I just have to make it through the night.

13
Night Terrors

I stay up late, working my way through the food, and making sure I've got all the pee and poo out of my body so that I don't have to leave my room until morning. After one last trip to the bathroom, I shut my bedroom door and, as quietly as I can, I pull my big chest of drawers across it, then angle my gaming chair between that and the leg of my bed so it's going to be proper hard to open from the outside. I wonder how many more doors I'll have to barricade before this is over. Then I leave empty crisp packets dotted around the floor. If someone was to get in, it'll be like walking through autumn leaves – they'll have no chance of sneaking up on me.

When I'm as sure as I can be that the room is secure, I check my CPAP over, strap on the mask and lie down on top of my duvet. I am bone tired. My legs are throbbing from all the jogging and creeping and stair climbing, and my eyes feel heavy and sore. When I close them, my brain screams at me to open them again. It doesn't matter how many times I tell myself that I'm safe as long as I have my CPAP on, the fear of turning into a sporeling, or of Mum getting into my room while I sleep, is almost overwhelming. Again, I think about making a run for it – away from Mum and the Christmas tree of doom downstairs. The urge to escape is so strong. But I force myself to calm down and think about the bigger picture – to think about everyone I care about and how I can help them. If I run, I'll probably get caught, either by Mum or whatever was looking for us at the golf course. And even if I don't, the hive will know I'm onto them and step up their game.

I don't know how long I lie there, exhausted but not asleep, my legs twitching and my mind shouting. And that's the thing about falling asleep – sometimes it can feel a million miles away, but it sneaks up on you without you noticing and your next thought is that it's light outside, or the alarm is ringing.

My next thought is that there's a noise above me – a noise that shouldn't be there. My eyes shoot open. It's still fully dark, and the inside of the house is quiet, apart from the familiar creak of the pipes, the gurgle of the radiators and the whirr of my CPAP. My phone is plugged in and lying on the desk next to my bed, cos even though I can't really use it for anything, it's just wrong not to keep it fully charged. I lean over and touch the screen. It's 3:59 a.m. As my eyes get used to the dark, I see that my barricade is as I left it, and I start to think I dreamt the noise. Then I hear it again.

It's a soft scratching, and it's moving slowly across the roof, like there's a sloth tiptoeing around up there, its claws scraping over the tiles. I pull down my CPAP mask and prop myself up on my elbows, staring at the ceiling like it's suddenly going to turn invisible and I'll be able to see what's up there. My first thought is that it's the thing we hid from at the golf course. But why would it be creeping across my roof? It's moved over my head now and towards the outer wall of the house where my bedroom window looks out over the street. The window. I have it open a lot because Mum keeps the house so hot. Was it shut? Was it locked?

The blind is only half pulled down, cos I never bother closing it properly when I'll just have to pull it up again in the morning. If you keep it at half, it's dark enough at night but you get enough light in the morning to get ready. Why give yourself extra work? I consider getting out of bed to make sure the window's secure, but I think I'm too late. From the scuffing against the guttering, I'd say that whatever was on the roof is now just above my window.

The heat of the house is so thick, it's like being smothered in a sleeping bag with the opening sealed up. I'm sweating everywhere, the beads of moisture feeling like insects crawling over my skin as they trickle downwards and drop onto the duvet. I remind myself to breathe.

My eyes are fixed on the window – a rectangle of faint light in the shadows of my room. The house opposite mine is dark and still, the XGen beacon on the roof reflecting the glow of a nearby streetlight. There are no lights from passing cars. No hum of distant traffic. All is silent and unmoving, like the moment before a shot is fired to start a race. Watching, listening and waiting.

I've almost convinced myself I was stressing over nothing when something eases into view from the top corner of the window: a black shape behind the blind, stretching slowly downwards. It's a human hand.

It comes into view as it reaches past the point where the blind ends. A hand, and an arm, inching down the glass like something out of a horror movie, fingers tiptoeing like spider legs. They stop at the window catch, and as they grip the edge of the frame, I see a flash of gold and green. And however bad I thought things were before suddenly shrinks into a first verbal warning, when I realise the gold and green is a ring – a ring I recognise. The thing on the roof is my mum.

As the hand – Mum's hand – claws and pulls at the window, a second hand and arm appear, followed by the outline of a head, with long dark strands of hair hanging towards the ground. My mum is crawling down the outside wall of my house, hanging upside down like a fly. It's the most awful thing I've seen in my life.

I hear the window catch give way as she pulls it with that steel grip she's developed. It creaks open a crack, then stops. She's listening to see if she's woken me. I wonder if she's holding her breath like I am, but I think probably not, seeing as she's a stone-hearted wasp creature who tries to force soup down my throat and can stick to walls. I only have a second to decide what to do. I'll never get past my own stupid barricade in time to get out of the room. I don't want to fight her, and I'm not sure if I even could. She's clearly super strong, and I don't have anything close that I can use as a weapon. So that leaves sticking to my original plan – playing along. As she pulls the window open further, a gust of that disgusting sweet smell hits my nose, and I pull my CPAP mask back up, lie down and close my eyes.

I feel the cold air from outside breezing into the room, but only for a moment, as another creak from the window cuts it short. She's inside, and she's closed the window behind her. I can't see, and I can't smell from beneath the CPAP mask, so I hope that means my hearing is temporarily enhanced. I need to know what she's doing in my room, and I need to be ready to move, in case she decides to try to murder me or, more likely, knock me out. I remember when we were on the coach driving into Crater Lake and Dale ran out in front of us, covered in blood. They'd attacked him; bashed him on the head so he'd fall unconscious. It worked.

After a few seconds of painful silence, I hear

her start to move. There's a sound like peeling Velcro heading towards me, but it's not coming across the floor, cos apparently that wouldn't be creepy enough. She's climbed back up the wall and is stalking across the ceiling, slowly and carefully. She doesn't want to wake me.

The noises stop right above my head. There's another silence where I imagine she's watching me. My whole body wants to shudder, but I focus on keeping my muscles relaxed, on breathing slowly. Picturing her above me, staring down with that creepy head tilt she's started doing is not helping me to be calm, so I try to picture peaceful things: turquoise oceans and summer skies; leaping dolphins and Christmas cookies. There's another peeling noise, like unsticking a plaster, and then quiet. I'm desperate to open my eyes to see what's happening, but I will them shut, imagining there are smooth, cool pebbles gently holding the lids closed. With the dolphins and the pebbles, I'm actually almost relaxed, and I make a note to do this next time I can't sleep cos my mind is too busy. Just as I'm finishing the thought, I feel something on my face, and it's lucky I'm totally chilled cos I manage not to leap out of bed screaming. It's only a tickle, like feathers brushing across my skin, but the urge to brush them away is freaking massive – like wanting to scratch a scab you've been told to leave alone or it will bleed out all over your designer tracksuit. What could it be? I picture Mum again, hanging off the ceiling like a creepy-ass chandelier, and realise – it must be her hair, falling down and touching my face. It could only reach, though, if she was standing vertically – her feet on the ceiling, but her hands not. So if her hands are loose, what is she doing with them?

Then I hear tapping, and the hiss of air escaping, and I know what she's doing. She's tampering with my CPAP. The CPAP is the only thing stopping me from turning into a sporeling. If it's compromised, I'll be breathing in the Christmas tree spores just like she did. And if I sleep, I'll become one of them. I feel panic creeping up, like when you remember in tutorial that you've got an assessment that day and you haven't done any revision. But worse, obviously, cos failing an exam means having to stay in at lunch and do it all over again, but turning into an alien bug means you'll be scuttling over rooftops, probably spitting poison, possibly growing freakish new body parts and definitely contributing to the fall of the human race. I really hate staying in at lunch, but this is at least two or three times worse.

You're not asleep, though, Lance, I tell myself. You won't turn if you're not asleep. And if she's going to the trouble of breaking my CPAP it means she's not going to hurt me. She's gonna make sure I'm breathing in those spores and that I'm fast asleep, then she's gonna leave.

So I focus on the endless friendly oceans. On the soothing pressure of the eye pebbles. On drifting on an inflatable with a cool drink in my hand. Something coconutty. And then the tickling stops and I listen as the Velcro hands and feet sneak back the way they came. The window creaks, and a gust of icy wind blows in, sweeping over me in a wave of refreshment and relief. It's flipping beautiful, man. The window closes and the scratching of Mum's vile insect hands and feet moves back up to the roof and over to the other side of the house. I open my eyes and lie in bed, waiting for morning.

14
Ade

I get dressed more quietly than I ever thought possible. Mum always says that when I move around in my bedroom, it sounds like a thunderstorm. I need to be out of the door before she knows I'm awake, because it's not going to take her long to realise I'm not connected to the hive mind. Right now, she thinks I'm sleeping and transforming and I need to keep it that way until I'm at a safe distance. I try to ignore the churning in my gut that's telling me I won't be able to come home again till this is all over. Today we need to fix everything, or there will be no chance for Straybridge.

As the morning chimes ring from St Anthony's, I run down the stairs and grab my coat. I put my shoes on by the front door, knowing I'll have to have one last conversation with Mum before I go. She appears, as I knew she would, and stands watching me with that tilted head and empty smile.

'Morning, Mum,' I say. 'Did you have a good sleep?'

'Did you?' she says.

'I got a few hours,' I smile. 'Could have done with a bit more, but I promised Kat I'd go to hers early. We're gonna get the others and then spend the day at hers.'

She frowns. Confused. 'I'd rather you stayed here.'

Yeah, so you can either sedate me or give me a nasty bump on my head and make sure the spores do their work. 'I promised, though,' I say. 'She wants me to help put their Christmas tree up. We're finally friends again and I don't want to ruin it.'

'You sure you're not too tired to be going out?'

'You know me, Mum,' I grin. 'I can go without sleep for days and still be amazing.'

'But it's nearly the big day,' she says, and I'm pretty sure she doesn't mean Christmas. What the hell is going to happen on the evil body-snatchers' Big Day? Something else to worry about once I get out of here.

So I say, 'Exactly. After today we'll be spending loads of time together at home.'

She frowns again. I know she's itching to go upstairs to find out why my vandalised CPAP didn't work as she thought it would.

'I really want to help Kat with her tree,' I say. 'Her mum hurt her arm playing netball, and her dad's got a shift, so they need help getting it into the living room.' I finish tying my lace. 'And I've thought about it, and because I don't exactly have muscles bursting out of my clothes and Kat's actually better at reaching the high branches than I am, I really think she just wants me to spend time with her.' I feel my face getting hot at that, because even though I'm making this up, the thought of it is like a mix of cringe and happy. 'I promise I'll stay home after today.' I stand up again and pull my coat on, reaching for the door handle as soon as my arm is in the sleeve. 'Could you do me a favour actually?' I add, as casually as I can manage. 'I think something might be wrong with my CPAP, cos I woke up about half four and it wasn't working properly. Could you check it for me, please?'

She looks at me like she's trying to read my

mind or count the number of freckles on my nose. She's concentrating. Assessing. I keep my face neutral as I zip up my coat. 'Of course,' she says, finally. 'I'll do that right now. Then hopefully you'll be able to rest better tonight.'

'Thanks, Mum,' I say. 'See you later.'

I open the door and have one foot outside when she calls me back. 'Just a minute, Lance.' I turn to see her walking down the hallway. 'I'm just getting something for you to take with you.' She disappears into the kitchen, and I wait for what feels like an hour, trying not to nervously jiggle on the front doorstep. Finally, she comes back with a travel mug. 'You haven't had breakfast,' she says. 'So I want you to make sure you have all of this good soup.'

'How did you make more soup?' I say, trying not to display my internal horror on my face.

'I can go without sleep for days, too,' she smiles. 'I got up early and wanted to keep busy.'

'Wow,' I say. 'You really are feeling better.'

She holds out the travel mug.

'Thanks,' I say. 'Feel free to start making chocolate cakes when you want to keep busy, though. Just saying.' I try not to let my hand shake as I reach towards her to take the mug, and I'm focussing so hard that it slips between my fingers – a genuine accident rather than another terrible way of getting rid of unwanted, potentially sedative, spit-laced soup. As both me and Mum fumble to catch it, her fingertips brush the back of my hand, and when I say brush, I mean like literally brush, because her fingers are so rough, they're like bristles scratching across my skin. Like the rough side of Velcro, in fact. 'Oh man,' I say, as I get a grip on the mug before it hits the floor. 'That was close. Lucky we both have lightning reflexes.'

She's looking at me in that way again, like she's trying to see into the depths of my soul.

'Would you mind if I share this with Kat?' I say. 'I'll feel weird having it all to myself in front of her.'

'Why not,' Mum says. 'The more the merrier, as they say.'

'Exactly.' I'm a few steps up the path now. I see Betty hiding behind the bins and I try to tell her with my eyes not to venture into the house. 'Cheers, Mum. See you later.'

Then I turn, and walk, and I don't look back.

Kat's ready and waiting when I get to hers a few minutes later. It doesn't look like she slept much either – there are dark circles around her eyes, and she's yawning like a sleepy squirrel.

'Thank goodness you're alright,' she says as she opens the door and hugs me. 'I was so worried. How was it with your mum?'

'Oh man,' I say. 'Probably, no, definitely, the worst night of my life. Let's get going and I'll fill you in.'

We walk to Karim's to pick him up like we promised. He actually looks like he's had the best night of his life. 'Totally crashed out,' he says. 'Got, like, ten hours of solid shut-eye. Mum never came back. Dad wasn't too worried because she said she might have to pull an all-nighter, but he's going to take her in some lunch after he's been shopping. Hopefully they won't let him in the building either.' He makes a face. 'Otherwise I'll never be able to go home again.'

'Hey, me and you can be hobos together,' I say. 'Cos I'm not going back to mine.'

'We could sleep under the bridge where it smells of pee.' Karim grabs his pouch, shuts his front door behind him and we make our way across his drive.

'Or you could both just sleep at mine,' Kat says. 'Idiots.'

We walk through the estate without trying to hide, knowing that everyone watching – and they are watching – will just see that we're doing exactly what we said we'd be doing. So we laugh and chat like it's a normal day, and ignore the side-eyes from dogwalkers and faces that peep at us from windows.

'We're going straight to Mak's, right?' Kat says. And it's so awkward because she knows where we're going first, and it's the last place she wants to be.

'We need her,' I say. 'And underneath it all, she's still Ade.'

'Is she though?' Kat says. 'She's like a totally different person and I doubt she'll want to help us.'

'She's the smartest person we know,' I say. 'She's brave and loyal, and she'd do anything for her friends.'

'Are we talking about the same Ade that goes to Latham?' Karim snorts.

'You see?' Kat says. 'Karim knows.'

'Look,' I say. 'What we went through at Crater

Lake was nothing compared to starting high school. We've all made bad decisions. We all forgot what was important. I don't know why Ade changed like she did, but I know there will be a good reason for it, and I know that if we ask her for help, she'll help.'

Kat huffs, but keeps walking in the direction of Ade's house, so I take that as a win. Ade lives on the big road that makes up one of the borders of Karim's estate, so we cut through Two Rivers on a rough diagonal, weaving in and out of the little cul-de-sacs, leaving curtains twitching behind us. I'm acting like I'm sure everything's gonna be ok, but when we get there, I'm nervous to knock on Ade's door. And for totally different reasons from when I was scared to knock on Kat's. But Karim's never really met her, and Kat's not gonna do it, so I step forward and knock. With fake confidence.

Ade's mum answers the door, holding Ade's baby sister, Callie. She's got so much bigger since I last saw her, which makes me a bit sad. Her face is covered in dribble and what looks like Bolognese. Neither of them look especially buggy. 'Lance and Katja!' She looks totally surprised to see us. 'I didn't know you guys were all friends again.'

'We're not,' Kat says, tickling Callie and making her chuckle.

'But we're hoping to be,' I add.

'Well, if anyone can get through to her, it's you.' Ade's mum smiles. 'And I don't think we've met?' She looks at Karim.

'This is Karim, a friend from school,' I say. 'I hope you don't mind us coming over.'

She opens the door and steps back to let us through. 'Oh god no, it's great to see you, especially if you can talk some sense into Adrianne.'

I go in first, wiping my feet on the mat, and walking through into their front room where Ade's other brothers are having a pretty violent game that involves volcanos and dinosaurs.

'Just ignore the twins,' Ade's mum says. 'They're having one of those days. They've already broken a chair and knocked the Christmas tree over.'

Ade's house is always chaotic and messy. There's stuff literally everywhere cos they don't have enough room for everything, and it's full loud all the time. They're all crammed in together, so they argue a lot, but they also have the most fun. I used to love coming here. I'm relieved to see that their Christmas tree is a plastic one, covered in homemade decorations. No spores here.

'She's up in her room, as you can probably hear.' Ade's mum closes the door behind us. 'Go up, and see if you can get her to turn the music down.'

'Thanks,' I say, and start up the stairs, with Kat and Karim behind me.

'Oh, sorry, do you want a drink?' she calls from the kitchen.

'We're good, thanks,' I call back, as we reach the top of the stairs and then turn right onto a second load of steps that lead to the attic. Well, it used to be an attic but it's a proper bedroom now, with a window and wallpaper – Ade's not Cinderella or anything like that. Her bedroom door is closed and music is blasting out. I knock loudly.

'I'm busy,' Ade's voice shouts from behind the door.

'Well, we tried,' Kat says. 'Let's go.'

I knock again. 'Ade, it's me, Lance.'

There's a pause when I wonder if she's heard me, and then the music gets quieter and the door opens. Ade is standing there looking so different from six months ago Ade. And it's not just the clothes – the spotless Nike Air Force Ones, the top that looks wrong for the freezing cold weather, or the make-up – the black eyebrows and giant eyelashes. Her hair is pulled up tight in a massive dollop on top of her head – I have no idea how girls get their hair to stay like that. It's something about the way she's standing, and the look on her face.

'What are you doing here?' she says to me. 'And you can get out of my house right now.' She looks at Kat like she's a walking piece of poo that's just smeared itself up the stairs.

'I'm out,' Kat says, turning to leave.

'No,' I say. 'Please, Kat.'

'This is what Katja does,' Ade says. 'Ditches people the moment things get real.'

'This is what Ade does.' Katja spins back to face Ade. 'Says vile things to people to distract attention away from her chav earrings.'

'Oof,' Karim says.

'Who even are you?' Ade turns on Karim. 'And why are you getting in my business?'

'Guys!' I'm gutted that things got this bad this fast. 'Please just stop.'

Ade glares at me. 'Why do you keep interfering, Lance? Always trying to be the hero to make up for the fact that you suck at everything.' And I get that she's raging about a bunch of stuff I don't understand, but it stings a little.

'What happened to make you turn into such a cow?' Kat says, standing a little closer to me, like my personal bodyguard. 'I knew we shouldn't have come here.'

'I never asked you to,' Ade shouts. 'Get the hell out.'

'They're back,' I shout. 'The spores, Ade. They're here in Straybridge.'

She looks at me like this might be part of a crazy scheme to get the gang back together. 'They can't be.'

'His mum's already turned,' Kat hisses at her. 'He had to spend last night in the same house with her while she tried to feed him soup, climbed over the roof and in through his bedroom window at four a.m. and hung upside down from his ceiling to damage his CPAP while he was sleeping so that he'd turn too. And after all that, he thought we should come to you to make sure you're OK.'

'And to see if you'll help us,' I add, because that's the truth, and it feels dishonest to say I'm only there to be kind.

Ade looks from Kat to me, and back again, her face unreadable. For about thirty seconds, no one says anything. I hear Ade's music rumbling on – the kind I'm not allowed to listen to at home cos of all the swears. Every now and then one of the twins roars so loudly downstairs that it echoes up to us. It sounds dumb but until this moment, I have never doubted that Ade will come through for us. I hope this is gonna go the way I want.

'Your mum is one of them?' she says. 'Hunter or worker?'

'They're different this time,' I say. 'There aren't workers like there were at Crater Lake. The people we've seen that have changed have been something else.'

'I'm sorry, Lance,' Ade says. 'I can't imagine what you've been through, and I shouldn't have said that you suck at everything. You don't.'

'It's cool, Ade,' I say. 'But will you help us? We know quite a bit, but there are gaps – things we can't work out. We could really do with a smart-arse like you.'

'Of course I'll help.' She goes back into her room and switches off the music. 'You'd better tell me everything.'

'We'll tell you on the way,' I say, 'to get the others.'

Ade sighs. 'Do we have to go to his house?'

'We're not leaving anyone behind,' Kat says. 'Whatever's happened between you and him doesn't matter. If I can get over things enough to come here, then you can get over whatever beef you have with Mak. We'll get Chets first, and then we're going to Mak's.'

I literally have no idea what beef they're referring to. Karim looks at me and I shrug.

'Fine,' Ade says. 'Let's go.' She grabs her puffy coat from her room and we all walk down the stairs. Well, me and Karim walk, and Ade and Kat stomp. There's a pretty awkward silence.

'My mum's turned, too, in case anyone cares,' Karim says. 'Just putting that out there.'

And I probably shouldn't, but I snigger cos the way he says it is just funny. Then Kat snorts out a laugh, and Karim grins.

Ade still has a face like stone. 'Who did you say this is, Lance?'

'Wow.' Karim's grin falls off his face. 'Tough crowd.'

15
Chets and Mak

Of course it would be easier to wait till we get to Mak's house to go through everything that's happened when everyone's together, but Ade wants answers and I can understand that, so we talk as we walk and try not to leave anything out. Well, I say we, but it's mostly me. Kat's still mad and I think Karim is scared of Ade. Which is another thing I can understand. Ade interrupts every now and then to ask questions, but she mostly just listens.

Chets lives the furthest away: across the river, out the back of the estate, through the posh residential area and across Cygnet Park. I feel like I've walked a million miles over the past two days, but there's no way we're doing this without Chets. We enter the park by the entrance furthest away from Chets' house and make our way across past the pond, which has been abandoned by the swans. It's funny how the birds seem to know about the spores before anyone else does and get their asses away fast. We're passing the playground when I see a familiar person jumping off a swing, waving like a madman.

'It's Chets!' I say, so happy to see him that I almost wave like a madman back.

'Aw, look at his happy face,' Kat says, grinning.

'Strange that he's appeared in the right place at the right time,' Ade says. 'A little bit suspicious, don't you think?'

'I'm sure there's a reason,' I say. Having Chets around makes everything better, and I can tell just from looking at him being all goofy as usual that he most definitely isn't a sporeling.

'Yeah, Adrianne. You've turned mean,' Kat says, and she pulls open the playground gate, running across the spongy ground to hug him. As the rest of us get closer, I look Chets over, just to double-check that he hasn't changed. He's all neat, his cheeks are pink and his eyes are like balls of chocolate. Same old Chets.

'Fancy meeting you here,' Ade says, raising an eyebrow.

'I can't believe it!' Chets beams, oblivious to the

shade Ade's throwing. 'I finally persuaded Mum and Dad to let me out of the house because I thought I was getting a vitamin D deficiency and my knees felt strange.'

'You see, Adrianne,' Kat says, linking arms with Chets.

'I was just thinking about walking to your house, Lance, but here you are! Were you coming to knock for me? It's so great to see you all together,' Chets says. And I see that he's avoiding looking at Karim.

Better get it over with. 'Chets,' I say. 'This is my friend Karim, from Latham. I've told you about him.'

'Aw, you've been talking about me?' Karim says in a cutesy voice that's really annoying. 'All good things, I hope?'

'Not *all* good things,' Chets says. 'There was something about a misdemeanour in the lab.'

'What?' Karim says, and for a second my belly lurches, wondering how Chets could know what we got up to in the lab yesterday.

'I believe it involved a Bunsen burner, a chemistry text book, and a shocking lack of respect for health and safety.'

Karim and I start laughing. There was an incident in the chemistry lab at school a few weeks ago that resulted in Karim getting a weekend detention. 'Oh, that,' he says. 'Yeah, I got in a bit of trouble for that one, but it was mostly an accident.'

'How could it be mostly an accident?' Chets says.

'Be nice, Chets,' I say. 'You're my friend, and Karim is too, and I know you'll like each other once you've spent some time together.'

'Oh god!' Ade rolls her eyes. 'You're acting like a bunch of Year Sixes. Let's just get going. Alien invasions are a bit more important than your pathetic jealousy.' And she stomps up the road ahead of us.

'You see,' Kat says. 'Mean.'

'What was that about alien invasions?' Chets says, looking like he probably looked when his mum made him sleep in a bed with her the other night.

'Don't worry, we'll catch you up,' I say. 'But Ade is right – we should keep moving.'

Mak lives on the same road as Ade, but all the way up the other end, backing onto Straggler's

Fields, which we take a short-cut through on the way to Latham. They're vast – stretching all the way to where the train tracks meet the motorway, and have been another place we've spent a fair bit of time when we're doing things we're not really supposed to be doing. It's a long walk and we're slower because Chets likes to take the cheerful route through life and stop to admire holly bushes and the new extension someone's built a few roads over. Then that moves on to people's Christmas light displays and, frustrating as it is, it does help with our aim of looking normal to any of the hive mind that might be watching. It's also one of the things I like most about Chets – in his eyes, kittens are fluffier, the sunshine is brighter and people are kinder. It's nice to look at the world through them from time to time.

When we get to Mak's, I get that door-knocking fear all over again. Mak and his family are hardcore preppers and experts at survival. They literally spend half their lives preparing for the end of the world, so that if the apocalypse comes they can handle themselves. If they've turned, we'll be in trouble for sure. But time is ticking, so I step forward and knock.

Mak's dad looks dead happy when he sees it's us. 'Kids, it has been a long time. You are welcome here, come in, come in.'

We follow him into the living room where Mak's little sister Zuzie is watching TV and Mak's mum is working on a computer. Their Christmas tree stands in the corner by the front window, looking brilliantly not like a Crater Lake tree. It's thinner, and a different shade of green. 'Lovely tree,' Kat says, as Mak's mum looks up and beams at us.

'Thank you.' Mak's dad smiles. 'We cut it down ourselves from place in mountains. Lithuanian tradition.'

'Is Maksym here?' I ask.

'He is spending lot of time in annex,' Mak's mum says. 'He's, erm, hard work for weeks. But now you come, you cheer him, yes?'

'We'll try,' Kat says. 'Can we go over to the annex, please?'

'Yes, yes.' Mak's dad smiles again. 'I will let you out through back door. Go to end of garden, then follow path through trees, and there you will find it.'

'There is food in kitchen there,' says Mak's mum. 'You please to take what you want.'

'Thanks so much,' I say. Mak's parents are so nice, and not at all what you'd expect if you knew what they got up to every summer. I heard Mak's mum can shoot a bird through the eyeball with an arrow from like a mile away.

We follow Mak's dad to the back door and make our way across the garden. Mak's house is so normal – semi-detached, three bedrooms, creaky stairs and a broken tap in the downstairs toilet that squirts boiling water at you if you touch it. But the annex is something else. I've only ever seen it from the outside, but it's all glass and wood and automatic shutters. I'm excited to go inside. At the end of the garden is a black wooden gate that opens into the woods that run down the side of Straggler's Fields. Mak's family own a big chunk of land which is fenced off from the rest of the fields. It feels like you're stepping into another world.

The path winds through the woods a short way and opens out into a clearing. The annex is just suddenly there, in front of you, like it's part of the forest. When Mak has family over from Lithuania, they stay in the annex, but his parents let him sleep out here sometimes, too. It's big –

maybe the length of a couple of trucks, with a circular bit at one end, and a rectangular structure coming off that. The circle part has floor-to-ceiling glass all the way around it, which looks luxurious, but I think is more to do with being able to see in every direction, cos they call it the Lookout. From where we're standing, I can see Mak slumped on the sofa in the middle of the Lookout, shoving handfuls of crisps into his mouth while watching TV.

'You can go first, Lance,' Karim says, as we all look at Mak like we're watching a sad gorilla in the zoo. He looks like he hasn't changed his clothes in a while, and his normally super-short hair has got longer, and messy. It's not long enough to cover that earring, though – the diamond in it is so big that I can see it winking at me from here. I crunch across the ground towards the door, half afraid that it's protected by tripwires and automatic weapons. I'm still a few metres away when Mak jumps up off the sofa, and looks out at me. I wave and mouth 'hi' and I really don't know what his reaction is going to be. I haven't spoken to him in a while. His gaze drifts behind me to the others, and then down to his stained, crusty clothes, and he looks gutted. But he walks over to the door, and opens it.

'What are you guys doing here?' he says. 'Something's happened, hasn't it?'

'Yeah, something's happened,' I say. 'Look, I know you're busy with other stuff, but we could really use your help.'

'Of course,' he says. 'Come in.'

I turn and nod to the others, and they follow me into the annex. Mak rushes over to the remote control to turn the TV off, but not before I see that he's watching a Christmas love movie, like the ones my mum likes. Mak really has changed.

Me, Kat, Karim and Chets squash onto one sofa, while Ade perches on the edge of a chair. Mak just stands there, and there is the most awkward silence ever, as nobody knows what to say.

'You alright, Mak?' Chets chirps up after a painful minute. 'How's things?'

'Yeah, you know, same old. You?'

'All good. Just rollin' with my homies.'

This obviously makes me laugh, and Karim and Kat too. Mak smiles, and the corner of Ade's mouth flicks up a tiny bit like she's trying not to smile too.

'What?' Chets says. 'I've gotten more street since I've been at high school.'

'I've missed you, Chets.' Kat puts her arm around him and squeezes him.

'So, what's going on?' Mak sits on the rug and crossed his legs. 'I'm guessing it's bad.'

'So bad,' says Kat. 'Straybridge has been infiltrated by the alien bug creatures from Crater Lake.'

'Can't say I'm surprised,' Mak says, with the look of an old man who's been through a few things in his time. 'It was inevitable. There were too many loose ends after Crater Lake and, if something like that can happen once, it's only a matter of time before it happens again.'

It's funny – you'd think an alien invasion would be shocking, but it seems like we were all expecting it, except for Karim obviously, and he's dealing like a pro.

'You got any snacks?' Karim says.

'Yes, snacks,' says Kat. 'We definitely need snacks.'

'Kitchen's through there, in the Tail.' Mak points at an open doorway that leads into the rectangle part of the building. 'There's loads in the cupboards and fridge. Why don't you bring out some stuff for everyone while I'm catching up?'

'Am I good to take whatever?' Karim says, already unsquashing himself from the sofa.

'Yeah, anything,' Mak says. 'Oh, except the unlabelled glass jars in the fridge with different-coloured liquids in them. You don't want to touch those.'

'Right,' Karim says, raising an eyebrow.

'Can you show us around?' Chets says. 'This place is awesome.'

'Chets, we don't have that much time,' I say.

'Please? It's not that big, and we can talk while we're doing it.' He bounces out of the seat, ready to go.

I have to admit, I'm desperate to look around, too. 'OK, but we need to be quick.'

So Mak shows us around the annex and it is even cooler than I thought it would be. The Lookout is eighty per cent glass-walled, so it's almost like sitting in the actual woods. There's a ladder-like staircase at the back that leads up to a platform where you can walk all the way around the circle and see out across the forest and fields. The floor of the circle is wooden, but with a circular rug in the middle where the sofa, table, TV and chairs are. Opposite the ladder to the platform, there is a doorway that leads into the Tail, which is a long, narrow rectangle. As we walk through the opening, I see we're in a kitchen area, with all the normal kitchen stuff running along the wall on our left. About a third of the way down the Tail, the corridor narrows and there are doors going off either side. On the left there's a toilet and shower room, and on the right there's a bedroom, which has an unmade bed, and dirty clothes all over the floor. Mak goes red and stuffs something under the duvet.

'Sorry, wasn't expecting anyone to visit.'

At the end of the corridor is another door, leading to an impressive storage room. I've never really thought of storage rooms in this way before, but here we are, and things change. It has deep freezers, shelves and shelves of canned foods, matches, toothpaste, sleeping bags and a bunch of stuff I don't recognise. There are metres of ropes looped on the walls like cowboys' lassos, with tools and what look like grappling hooks all hanging neatly from racks.

'Woah,' Karim says. 'I know where I'm coming when the zombies arrive.'

'This isn't even the best part,' Mak smiles. 'You should see downstairs.'

'There's a downstairs?' Kat says.

'The bunker,' Mak says. 'Built to withstand multiple end-of-the-world scenarios.'

And I am dying to see it, but we need to get Mak up to speed, so we head back to the Lookout while Karim prepares the snacks.

Mak becomes more like his old self as we fill him in on everything that's happened. We used to do this all the time – chat together for hours. If Ade wasn't sitting on her own, throwing everyone evils, it would almost be like old times. I wish I knew the way to make things right between her and Kat, cos I feel like if they made up, she'd be OK with the rest of us, too. Mak glances over at Ade every now and then, and then immediately looks away. Kat helps me tell the story, adding bits when I forget them, and Chets sits in silence, listening.

When we've finished, and Karim has brought in a proper, top picnic, Mak says, 'So what's the plan?'

16
Unravelling

'You don't have enough facts to make a plan,' Ade says. 'Well, not one that will work anyway.'

'Very helpful,' Kat snarks back. 'Do you want to tell us what additional facts we need so that we can get to a point where we can make a plan?'

'First of all,' Ade sighs. 'You're glossing over a key detail: why hasn't Karim's tree affected him in the way Lance's has changed his mum?'

'We thought maybe it was too small?' Karim half whispers, like he's talking to an angry tiger.

'Does it have the cones on it?' Ade says.

'Yes.'

'The spores will be coming from the cones, because they're the galls formed by the parasites. If there are cones, there are spores, so being small isn't relevant.'

'What else is different about your tree, Karim?' I say. 'Have you not been close to it very much?'

'You know I'm in that room all the time, mate,' he says. 'And I stand right next to that tree to do my hair.'

'Jeez, then you're clocking up a lot of contact hours,' I say.

'Exactly,' says Karim. 'Perfection takes dedication. And a lot of hairspray.'

'Hairspray!' Ade says. 'Do you spray your hair next to the tree?'

'Only four or five times a day.'

'PVPs,' Ade says. 'That could do it.'

'PVPs?' I know I sound like an idiot, but I really have no idea what she's talking about.

'Sticky synthetic polymers.' Mak nods. 'I think you're right, Ade, they could be creating a hard barrier on the galls.'

'Come again?'

'The hairspray is coating the cones with a sticky residue that prevents the spores from being released,' Ade says. 'That's why Karim hasn't turned.'

'Ah, she actually used my name,' Karim says and draws his finger down his face in a fake teardrop. 'Did you hear that, guys?'

Kat giggles.

'Ade, you're brilliant,' I say.

'Yeah, well,' she sniffs, but again I can see she's trying not to smile.

'So now we have a way of neutralising all the Crater trees in town,' I say, feeling, like, proper smug.

'But there are still all the other unanswered questions.' Ade again.

We all look at her.

'If the spores are coming from the trees, and the trees are all over Straybridge, why isn't everyone being turned?'

'I'm assuming you're only asking us because you already know the answer, and you want to make us feel stupid,' Kat says.

Ade rolls her eyes. 'The truth hurts sometimes, Katja.'

'So,' I say, impatient to hear more, 'do you know why everyone hasn't turned?'

'I expect that the concentration of spores is weaker,' Ade sniffs. 'In Crater Lake we were surrounded by spores directly from the meteor. The tree galls aren't the original spores – they're a mutated version. They could be less potent, have a smaller range of spread, or be slower acting.'

'So they only change people who are close to them over a certain amount of time,' I say.

'And who don't have an extensive hair-styling routine.' Karim pats his hair.

'If the cones are the galls,' I say, a stab of dread poking at my gut. 'Would it make a difference if they were open or closed?'

'I'd say so,' Mak says. 'What are the cones like?'

'At the moment they're like the size of satsumas, round and made up of loads of woody petals that are curled into each other, like the bud of a flower,' I say.

'That's a very good description, Lance,' Kat smiles at me. 'That's exactly what they're like.' It makes me embarrassingly pleased with myself.

'So they're definitely closed?' Mak asks.

'I would say so.' I nod. 'Mum said, before she changed, that they'd open in a few days and that they'd release a nice smell. Supposedly.'

'So when the cones open,' Kat says, 'it's not going to be just a smell coming out.'

'We have to stop it from happening,' I say. 'The spore situation we've had so far is just the start – easing us in. When they open there'll be no stopping them.'

'What are you going to do, Lance?' Ade says. 'Raid the shopping centre for cans of hairspray and run from house to house coating each individual tree with PVPs? It's not possible.'

'Oh man,' I say. Cos she's right. Even if we knew where all the trees were, how would we get access to them all? And without the swarm stopping us.

'You'd better make a plan B,' Ade says, sipping on her coke.

And I don't really like her cruddy attitude right now, but she is annoyingly bang on. We need a change of direction. 'Any thoughts on the glitching situation with Mum?' I say.

'Tell us exactly what happened,' Mak says.

'So she glitched the night after the explosion, and that's definitely when she changed. Up till then she was Mum. I mean I think she'd been changing physically – she was well and full of energy, like I haven't seen her for years. But she was still my mum. Then she glitched in the middle of the night, and totally changed.'

'What time did you say that was?' Ade asks.

'It was at four a.m., the first night of curfew.' And even as I'm saying it out loud, the scraps of information I've been keeping in my head start to connect. 'The same time that Hoche said the XGen signal went down.'

'Do you believe Hoche?' Chets asks. 'I mean, and please don't take this the wrong way, but she didn't like you at Montmorency. Why would she help you?'

'She didn't say it like she was trying to help us,' Kat says. 'It was more accidental than that.'

'Unless she knew what you were up to and was trying to misdirect you,' Chets says.

'You think she's one of them?' I frown. And it fits like one of her awful shoes – she's exactly the sort of person who would use her cunning to throw us off the scent.

'Do you remember what she said back at Crater Lake, about how she'd make the perfect queen bee?' Mak says.

'And we don't know for sure if she ever properly turned back. She left Montmorency straight after, and we never saw her again,' I say.

'She could have been one of them the whole time,' says Kat.

'But didn't she help you get into the university building?' Ade says.

'Not on purpose,' I say.

'Or was it?' Ade raises an eyebrow.

Chets reaches for a pizza slice. 'Well, she wouldn't have been helping Lance, would she? It doesn't make sense.'

'I'm confused,' Kat sighs and rubs her eyes.

I am too. I felt like we were making progress, but now things are even more mixed up than before. 'OK,' I say. 'Let's consider for a minute that what Hoche said was true – that the XGen signal cut at four, which is the exact same time my mum glitched. What would that mean?'

'It would mean that the removal of the signal was connected to your mum becoming full alien,' Mak says.

'You say you believe they can all communicate with each other through their minds, and from what I've heard, that sounds plausible,' Ade says, sounding more and more like the old Ade with each passing moment. 'If that's the case, and they are all connected to some sort of hive mind, perhaps it only activated at that moment – four a.m. on the night of the explosion, and that's why your mum's behaviour changed so suddenly.'

'The XGen signal was preventing the hive mind from connecting,' I say.

'Maybe the phone and data signals get in the way of the messages going between the bugs.' Kat claps her hands. 'And the microwaves.'

'It's probable that any waves affect their communication,' says Ade. 'Microwaves, radio waves, digital data waves...'

'That would mean they'd really want to get XGen turned off,' Kat says.

'There were XGen beacons in the alien labs,' I say. 'Maybe they're testing them for weaknesses, to find the best way to destroy them.'

'They are properly difficult to damage,' Karim says, 'without doing something drastic, like running them over with a truck or hitting them with lightning.'

'Know your enemy,' Mak says, 'and you'll know how to defeat them.'

'Exactly,' I say.

'But, if that's true, why would they choose this town to start their global takeover?' Chets says. 'It doesn't make sense when it would be easier somewhere else.'

'Because the world is watching,' Ade says.

'Nothing ever happened in Straybridge before the SMARTtown investment,' I say, and I'm getting excited, cos this really does add up. 'And now we're the first to get XGen and everyone else is waiting to see how well it works.'

'If it fails here, nobody will want it,' says Mak.

'And the rest of the world will be easier for them to invade.' Kat gasps, her blue eyes wide and bottomless, like those pools you see in movies where the water in them gives people eternal life.

'If they stop XGen in Straybridge, they stop it completely,' Ade says. 'And I'm sure the fact that the group of people who defeated them at Crater Lake live in Straybridge is another incentive. We know better than anyone else how to fight them.'

'If they make us part of the hive mind, they take out their strongest opposition,' I nod.

'I've moved into the actual hellmouth,' Karim says.

'But at least you have us.' I grin.

'I mean, I have you, and I've possibly won over Kat. Mak might grow to love me in time, but Ade and Chets definitely hate me. So that's a mixed bag at best.'

We all laugh, and it feels so great to be sharing this with these people. My people. But then Chets says, 'Does this mean Ade and Kat have made up?' And the laughing comes to an awkward end.

'No chance,' Ade says, throwing a look of poison at Kat.

Kat stares back, her face a brewing storm.

And I know this needs sorting out before we can do anything else. So I take action, even if it means losing Kat again.

'Right,' I say. 'We can't fight the spores if we're fighting each other. Everyone knows that – it's in every movie ever made and things don't become massively predictable storylines unless there's some truth in them in the first place. We're having this out, here and now.'

17
A Start

'Is there time for me to pee first?' Karim says. 'I don't want to miss anything.'

'Just go,' I say, and he literally runs off into the Tail, faster than I've ever seen him move before.

'Are you sure this is a good idea?' Mak says, looking from Kat to Ade as they face off across the coffee table.

'You could always run off to your girlfriend if it's uncomfortable for you,' Ade snaps.

Mak looks hurt. 'Why are you bringing that into it? I thought this was about you and Kat.'

'To be fair, mate,' I say. 'And I'm only speaking for myself here, but I've found it hard that you haven't been around since you got with Georgia-Rae.'

'Lance is right,' Kat says. 'You just ditched us when she came along, like we didn't matter to you at all. It was a jerk move.'

'Just because you two are suddenly friends again doesn't mean you have to team up,' Mak says, as Karim runs back into the Lookout.

'Aw, I've missed stuff,' he says. 'That sucks.'

'Why are you here?' Chets says, getting up off the sofa and turning on Karim. 'You're not part of our group and you never will be.'

'Group – what group?' Ade laughs in a nasty sarcastic rather than happy way. 'We haven't been a group for months.'

'When did this all go so wrong?' I stand up too. 'We had the best summer, and then we started high school and everything fell apart.'

'Mak got a girlfriend and turned into an idiot,' Ade says.

'Ade started acting like some kind of gangster wannabe,' says Kat.

'And you started mixing with a bad crowd,' Chets says to me. 'You disappointed me, Lance. You could have been so much better.'

I knew he was a bit funny about Karim, but I didn't realise he thought I'd become a waste of space.

'First of all,' I say. 'Karim is not a bad crowd.'

'Thanks, mate.' Karim holds up his knuckles,

and I feel like it's not the time, but I'm not going to air him in the current circumstances, so I try to bump fists in a quick and non-smug way because I think Chets might explode.

'When we started high school, I thought it was going to be great,' I say. 'It felt like a chance to be someone new, like I could forget about Hoche and Trent and start again. But it wasn't like that at all – it was just as hard as primary but in new, worse ways. I lost all my friends, one by one, and I didn't have a clue why. Mum got really ill and it was my fault. Karim's been there for me when none of you have.'

'How is it your fault about your mum?' Kat says.

And this is it – the guilt I feel all the time. 'She first got ill when she was pregnant with me,' I say. 'So ill that she couldn't have another baby, even though I know she wanted one. She and Dad split up over it, so technically that was my fault, too.'

'No way, Lance,' Ade says. 'Your mum's illness is not your fault, and neither is your dad leaving. That was between them – people can have worlds of problems going on that you don't know about, even if you're close to them.'

'And your mum loves you so much,' Kat says. 'If she could go back in time and choose – to either have you and her illness along with it, or to be well all the time and not have you, what do you think she'd say?'

And I know what she'd say, so I don't answer cos I feel stupid and embarrassed.

'You make her happier than her illness makes her sad,' Kat says. 'And I'm sorry that I wasn't there for you when you needed me.'

'Me too,' Mak says. 'I got a bit carried away.'

I look at Chets, hoping he'll back me. What he said hurt, but we've been through so much together that I'm not gonna hold a grudge. I haven't always done right by him either.

'Remember when you wanted to stop me from being friends with Trent?' Chets huffs. 'Because you thought I was too good for him?'

'Yeah,' I say. 'Because you are.'

'This is the same as that.'

'It's not. Karim is not like Trent.'

'Seems very similar to me.' Chets folds his arms.

'Wait, are we talking about that goon from your last school who was basically the worst human being on the planet?' Karim says.

'That's the one.' Ade picks at a thread on her chair so hard that one of her plastic nails pings off.

'You know I'm really starting to regret coming along today,' Karim says. 'And it's not even because of the risk of dying or becoming an alien.'

Kat puts her hand on Chets' arm. 'You know I think you're brilliant, Chets, but you're wrong about this – Karim isn't like Trent.'

'I'm pretty hopeful that there is only one Trent in the world,' I say. 'Cos that's more than enough. Karim is a good friend and a good person. Sure, he gets in trouble sometimes, but didn't I always do that, too? It didn't stop you from being my mate.'

'That was different,' Chets says.

'Why are you being like this?' I say. 'This isn't like you.'

'No, it isn't.' Ade raises an eyebrow again.

Chets looks at Ade, then at me again, and slumps into the seat a bit more. 'I'm just being cautious. It seems that he came to Straybridge at the same time that all this trouble started.'

'Because my mum works for XGen,' Karim says.

'That's very convenient, isn't it?' says Chets. 'Look, I'm just trying to protect Lance, that's all, in the same way that he protected me.'

'You're protecting him from the wrong thing, mate,' Mak says. 'The threat isn't in here, it's out there.'

And he points out of the glass door, just as someone comes pelting out of the trees.

18
Trent

'Let me in, losers!' Trent shouts, as he thumps on the door like he's trying to break it down, leaving sweaty smears all over the glass.

It's a face I haven't seen since July. Correction: it's a face I have loved not seeing since July. Although there have been loads of ups and downs since we left Montmorency, I can honestly say that not having Trent in my life has been constantly a Good Thing.

'What's he doing here?' Mak groans.

'We'll never know,' says Ade, 'because we're not letting him in.'

We all watch Trent as he carries on banging against the glass, like a fly on a lightbulb. 'It's me – Trent,' he says.

'Does he think we can't see him?' Kat asks. 'Because, you know, that's clearly glass he's pressing his face against.'

'Maybe he thinks we don't recognise him,' I say. 'High school changes people.'

'Idiots!' Trent hollers. 'Let me in right now or I'll smash up this conservatory.'

'But not Trent,' Ade sighs. 'Nothing changes Trent.'

'Should we let him in?' Karim says. 'I, for one, am fascinated to see how this develops.'

'I don't think that's a good idea,' says Chets. 'He looks desperate. People do crazy things when they're desperate. He could be dangerous.'

Trent is kicking and punching at the glass, leaving literally no damage on the door but clearly hurting his foot because he swears and starts hopping around. 'I'll Geek, Robot, Overlord you. If I win, you let me in.'

'Why not?' I call out to him. 'One, two, three...' and he calls Overlord, as he always does, at the same time as I call Robot. 'I win,' I say. 'Bye, Trent.'

'Best of three,' Trent says.

'What do you want, Trent?' Ade asks, standing with her hands on her hips.

Trent stops hopping and peers in through the glass. 'Adrianne, I didn't recognise you,' he calls, smoothing back his hair. 'You look good, girl.'

'Oh god.' Kat gasps, while Ade looks like she's being sick in her mouth and the rest of us crack up.

'We have to let him in now,' Karim says. 'He's like level-9000 entertainment value. Please?'

'You should listen to the kid with the hair,' Trent shouts. 'Let me in. We need to talk – there's some really weird stuff happening around here.'

'What sort of weird stuff?' I ask.

'Weird like Crater Lake,' he says. 'And I know something that you'll really want to know.'

'We're letting him in, aren't we?' Ade sighs again, sits down in her chair and pulls it further away from the door.

'I think we have to,' I say. 'We can just listen to what he has to say and then kick him out.'

Everyone makes a face, but no one objects, so Mak goes to the door and opens it. Trent falls into the Lookout, slams the door shut behind him and starts looking around the doorframe like a lunatic. 'Where's the lock?' he shouts. 'We need to make sure nobody else can get in.'

'It can't be opened from the outside,' Mak says. 'Otherwise you would have got in, wouldn't you?'

'Is it held shut with witch magic from your country?' Trent says.

'That's it. You can leave.' Mak opens the door again, at the same time as the rest of us make the sort of disgusted-slash-outraged noises that you'd expect to hear after a comment like that.

'Told you we shouldn't let him in,' Ade says.

'Wait!' Trent shouts. 'The information I have obtained is of great value. It might even save your lives.'

'Go on, then.' Mak sighs.

'Mind if I have a drink first?' Trent helps himself to a bottle of coke, opens it and gulps the whole thing back in one go. Well, I say the whole thing, but a fair bit of it dribbles down his chin. We all sit back down where we were before, which leaves no seat for Trent. He walks over to Ade. 'Mind if I share?'

'Yes,' she says. 'The floor's free if you really need to sit.'

Trent huffs about for a bit, but eventually grabs some pizza and sits on the floor. 'You guys are going to owe me for this,' he says.

'I seriously doubt it,' Kat says.

'Shut up freak girl, or I won't tell you.'

'For someone who desperately wanted to come in,' I say, 'you're doing a really good job of making us want to kick you out.'

'Alright, fine. Makes sense that if some mental stuff is happening in this town, it all leads back to you lot. That's all I'm saying.'

'What do you know, Trent?' Ade says.

'I'm not sure we should even listen,' Chets says. 'He'll probably lie.'

'Maybe,' I agree. 'But I think we should hear him out first, and then we can decide.'

'So, me and Madison have been staying at my grandma's for the last couple days...' He looks at Karim. 'FYI, Madison is my sister, new boy with hair. Anyway, we got dropped back today and straight away I thought my parents were acting even more uptight than usual. They kept trying to get us to go for naps, like we're toddlers or some shiz like that. Obviously not happening.' He pauses for another bite of pizza, then carries on talking while still chewing. 'They kept looking at each other in this way like they do when they're trying to hide something from me, and then they went through all the cupboards in the house, taking out all the cans of furniture polish and Lynx and stuff. They put it all in a bin bag, tied it up and put it in the loft. Then they sellotaped up the microwave, which was annoying because I wanted to make some Quick Chips.'

We all look at each other, which anyway is better than seeing the spitty cheese and tomato in Trent's mouth.

'Obviously I told them they were being idiots and to give me back my body spray, cos the girls love it.' He winks at Ade. 'They told me to go to my room, which I did, but then I snuck back down for food, and I heard them talking.' More loud, sloppy chewing. 'Mind if I have another coke?' He's already taken one before the question is even asked.

'What were they saying?' I ask.

'Ha!' Trent says. 'I knew you'd want to know. A lot of it was insane bleating on about protecting the vessels from being neutralised so close to completion, whatever that means.'

'It must mean when the cones are going to open,' I say. 'Did they say when completion is going to happen?'

'I don't know. It was so weird and boring. I was just wishing they'd get out of the kitchen so I could get to the cupboards.'

He's such hard work. 'Ade?'

'Think carefully, Trent,' she says. 'Did they mention anything about a timescale? A day that they're working towards.'

'They did say "after tomorrow, success will be inevitable".'

'Tomorrow!' Kat gasps.

'It's the day after today.' Trent rolls his eyes. 'Don't they teach you anything at scuzzy Latham High?'

'We learnt about days in Reception,' Kat says. 'You were there. We all were, remember?'

'Except me.' Karim puts his hand up. 'I didn't learn about days until Year One, at the same time that I learnt not to eat with my mouth open.'

'Anyway, most of it was dull as hell, but then they said something about Crater Lake, so I started listening properly. They were talking like they were there, but on Team Alien. It was all, "we were defeated in the crater, we cannot take any chances this time. At all costs" and I started thinking that maybe my mum and dad had breathed in the wasp fluff like what happened at Crater Lake. Then they said that the enemy from Crater Lake must be apprehended today, that those who posed the greatest threat were at the home of the boy called Maksym, and that they should prepare for battle.'

'This is bad,' Mak says.

'Yeah, so I got the hell out of there and came here to warn you losers. I figured if anyone had a plan to stop the creepy-ass bug people, it would be you freaks.'

'So you actually came here to help yourself,' Ade says. 'Typical.'

'What about Madison?' I say. 'Where's she?'

'Probably still at home, unless my parents have done something with her.'

'You left your little sister behind?' I say, and I'd love to say I can't believe it, but I actually really can.

'Have you seen her? She's stupid and slow. She would have taken too long and then I'd never have got away.'

'Classy,' Ade says.

'She'd have been no help anyway,' Trent says. 'She cries all the time and she's scared of the dark.'

'Isn't she, like, seven years old?' I say.

'Yeah, exactly.' Trent rolls his eyes. 'So I put myself at risk to come and warn you that, firstly, there are Crater Lake bug people in Straybridge, and secondly, they're coming for you. Like, soon.'

'And they know where we are,' I say. 'So we need to move.'

'We knew they'd know where we are,' Ade says. 'The interesting part is that they also knew about the hairspray, and the microwave, almost like they were listening in to our conversation.'

'Oh man,' I say, and my gut twists as I try to connect the dots.

'They could have worked it out for themselves,' Chets says.

'At the exact same time that we did?' I say. 'Nah, that's way too much of a coincidence.'

Kat looks around at everyone. 'But that means that one of us is…'

And it sickens me to think it, but we have to face facts. 'One of them.'

19
Bugged Out

We all jump out of our seats and back away from each other. Except Trent, who stays sitting on the floor eating pizza.

'None of us changed, though,' Kat says. 'We checked.'

'We must have missed something.' I look around the room at all the friends I've only just found again after months of missing them. Except that one of them isn't my friend. One of them is the enemy.

'I think it's obvious who the spy is,' Chets says. 'It has to be the person who we *know* has a Crater Lake Christmas tree in their house.'

'We saw Karim's mum change,' Kat says, 'and how it affected him. She changed in the labs, not at home.'

'That was yesterday, though,' Mak says. 'He slept at home again last night, so he could have turned between then and now.'

Karim has gone pale as he looks around at

everyone staring at him like he's a snake about to pounce. 'It isn't me,' he says. 'Lance, you know it isn't me.'

And I feel like a horrible person saying it, but at this point I can't trust anybody. None of us can. 'You did say you crashed out last night. That you had a really long, deep sleep. Maybe some sporage leaked out into your house after all, and did its work while you were unconscious.'

'Also,' Ade says. 'Your mum could have come home and knocked you out and put a new tree in your house.'

'My mum wouldn't knock me out,' Karim says.

'Yeah, she would, if she's one of them,' says Mak. 'Or she could have spat a sedative ball into your food.'

'She wouldn't even have needed to knock him out,' Kat says. 'She could have snuck in at any point and stuck a cone under his pillow while he was sleeping, like an evil, reverse tooth fairy.' She makes a face at Karim. 'No offence.'

'What about Chets?' Karim says. 'We didn't even see inside his house to know what kind of Christmas tree he has. And he just magically turned up in the right place at the right time.'

'Sounds like you're trying to pass the blame because you're guilty,' Chets says. 'And Lance knows that my mum always has a pre-lit, luxury, you-can't-tell-it's-not-real Christmas tree, because she doesn't like the mess of the needles dropping, and she hates getting scratched when she has to wind the lights around.'

'That's true,' I say. 'She does always have one of those.'

'You see,' Chets says. 'It's obviously you, Karim.'

Karim looks so hurt, and it makes me feel like a proper scumbag.

'To be fair,' Ade says. 'You've seemed rather unlike yourself today, Chetan. You're much more aggressive than usual, and I've noticed that you've been dragging things out all day, like you're trying to buy time.'

'Ade's right,' Mak says. 'Sorry, mate, but you have. You've been a jerk to Karim all day.'

'You're just siding with Ade because you like her,' Kat says. 'Madriak, the sequel.'

'That's snaky, Katja,' Ade says. 'Mak and I haven't even spoken to each other since he started going out with Georgia-Rae. He made it quite clear that he doesn't like me.'

215

'You've always got me, babe,' Trent says from the floor.

'Shut up, Trent,' Ade says.

'You know you're beautiful when you're mad,' says Trent.

'Where the hell have you been learning these lines, man?' Mak says. 'They suck butt.'

'I see,' Ade says. 'If someone says I'm beautiful, it must just be a line? Nice to know how you feel about me, Maksym.'

'I never said that.' Mak looks panicky. 'I just meant that they're new levels of cringe.'

'Not as cringe as you getting your ear pierced because your girlfriend told you to,' Kat says. And I'm completely confused because now she seems to be on Ade's side and I'm not sure what changed in the middle of this mental conversation.

'Guys, we're getting off the point,' I shout. 'We can keep accusing each other all day, and we're apparently just gonna drag up a load of other stuff.'

'As a tight friendship group, you guys have some serious issues to work through,' Karim says. 'No offence.'

'Man, don't say "no offence" when you mean offence,' Mak shouts.

'Kat said it to me when she was accusing my mum of being a creepy pixie, and no one cared about that,' Karim says.

'Everyone, shut up!' I yell, loud enough to shock them into silence. 'We need to find out who the bug is. Nothing else matters right now.'

'Is there a test we can do?' Ade says. 'Do you have any tardigrades, Mak? We could all eat some.'

'But Mak could tamper with whatever we're eating and give himself something different,' Chets says. 'No offence.'

'That's true,' I say. 'We wouldn't be able to trust the outcome. It needs to be something we can all see and believe.'

'So Chetan can say "no offence" and nobody complains,' Karim mutters. 'And what the hell is a tardigrade anyway? Once again, the new kid is out of the loop.'

'They're microscopic eight-legged creatures that are almost indestructible and can often be found living in wet environments, like in moss on riverbanks,' Kat says. 'We learnt about them at Crater Lake from this guy called Dale who was a scientist before he became an alien.'

'At Crater Lake we used them to turn the bugs

back into humans,' I say. 'Because the tardigrades consume the sporiness within the host bodies.'

'Right, got it,' Karim says. 'Those wrinkly mini hippos you showed me a picture of.'

'Ah, they are like wrinkly mini hippos,' Kat smiles. 'But with weird nose-mouths.'

'Like toothy vacuum-cleaner nozzles,' I say.

Karim nods and makes a face. 'And we want to eat these.'

'Actually, there's something I've been wondering about that,' I say, turning to Ade. 'If we eat tardigrades, we know they won't die, so does that mean we poo them out, or that they get absorbed into our bodies?'

'I expect we poo them out,' she says. 'Although it would be amazing if we could absorb them.'

'And take on their skills!' Karim says.

'We'd be like superheroes.' I'm totally thinking about seeing if this is possible. At a more convenient time, obviously.

'We can try this, right?' Karim asks me, and I can see he's as excited about it as I am.

'For sure,' I say, holding my hand up for a high five. Karim slaps it and we grin at each other, and then I have the best idea.

'That's it!' I say. 'That's the perfect test.'

'Experimenting on ourselves to see if we can turn into Tardi-Man?' Mak says.

I rub my fingers on the palm of my hand. 'My mum's hands are rough and sticky now. I think they're covered in something that helps her grip to the walls and hang upside down.'

'I know lots of insects have tiny bristles and claws to help them grip to surfaces,' Ade says. 'So that would make sense.'

'So, if we all high five each other, we'll know,' I say. 'If our hands are smooth and normal, it's all good; but if they're rough, we'll know we have an alien bug on our hands. Literally.'

'But I have the hands of a potato farmer,' Mak says, looking down at them like he's just got to the front of the dinner queue and they've run out of curly fries. 'They're hard and covered with callouses.'

'Hard and callousy is fine,' I say, although I'm not one hundred per cent sure what a callous is. 'Mum's hands were more scratchy – like the spiky side of Velcro.' I put my hand up for Mak to high five. He looks nervous, hesitates, and then does it. I don't notice the callouses as much as his super-strength which is annoyingly impressive, even when he's not trying.

'You're clear,' I nod. 'Karim, Mak, high five each other to confirm.'

They slap palms and both give a relieved nod.

'I'll go next,' Katja says. 'I have nothing to hide and I want to make sure you guys are all telling the truth.' She steps towards Mak, who puts his hand up and takes the high five and smiles. Then she fives Karim, and finally me. Not like I've been standing there waiting for it or anything. As her palm hits mine, I get a flashback to yesterday when we held hands for a bit because of the traumatic situation we were in. I figure it's good to think about, cos I can assess if there have been any skin changes since then. Her palms are soft and perfectly warm like the paw pads on a kitten. 'All good,' she smiles. 'Thank god for that.'

That leaves Ade and Chets.

'Guys,' I look from one to the other. 'You're up.'

'I'm not sure this is actually the most scientifically accurate test we could be doing,' Ade says.

'Ade's right,' Chets pipes up. 'We should find a better way.'

'We don't have time to come up with anything more scientifically accurate right now,' I say. 'And you have nothing to lose by giving it a try.'

'Five it, Ade,' Kat says, putting her hand up.

'Double five,' I say, putting mine up too.

Ade huffs and rolls her eyes. 'Fine.' She slaps both our hands a bit harder than is comfortable, if I'm honest. Then she walks over to Karim, who puts his hand up like he's sticking his head in a T-Rex's mouth. She fives him, then finally walks over to Mak and smacks his hand without making eye contact.

'Can everybody confirm that I don't have bristly insect hands?' She glares at us. We all nod. And that just leaves Chets. My heart sinks at the thought that he might be a sporeling, but then I think about how different he was when he turned at Crater Lake. If he's been spored this time, he's got much better at pretending. Which hurts more for some reason.

'This is a waste of time, Lance.' Chets backs up a couple of steps. And that makes me even more suspicious.

'Like I said to Ade, you have nothing to lose. We've all done it.'

'You know, it's possible that your mum just has something wrong with her hands.' He takes another step back and glances to his left and his right. 'You said she has weird side effects to her medications sometimes. Or she could have burnt them when she glitched with the kettle a couple of nights ago.'

'Maybe,' I say, stepping towards him. 'But it does add up – the way her skin stuck to my coat when she held my arm, and the noises I heard as she crawled across the ceiling. It makes sense that the surface of her hands has changed.'

'Come on, man.' Mak steps forward, too, his hand up and waiting. 'Just do it.'

'You'd be able to tell if I was a sporeling,' Chets says. 'I'd be acting out of sorts, like your mum.'

'I was there when my mum first activated,' I say, trying not to let a tear sneak into my eye cos I don't want to cry right now. 'And she was super weird. But as time went on, she sort-of got better at being like her old self. It's like she was learning.'

'Like new shoes,' Kat says. 'When you first put your feet in them, they're stiff and they hurt and they feel like they were made for someone else.

But then when you've walked around in them for a bit, they kind of mould to your feet and become part of you.'

'Yes, exactly like that, Kat! Great analogy.'

'Thanks,' she smiles.

'Except for any Nike Air Flyknits,' Karim says. 'Cos they are like joy on your feet fresh out the box. Just saying.'

'And the thing is, Chets.' I turn back to him. 'You've been turned before, so the hive already knows you, and your body knows how to be a sporeling.'

'He's like the hive mind's comfiest fluffy slippers,' Karim says. 'Am I right?'

'Too far, Karim,' I say. 'You took the analogy too far.'

'Yeah, it was smart when Kat said it,' Ade says. 'But you've ruined it now.'

Karim shuffles uncomfortably. 'Like I said, tough crowd.'

'So Chets, just high five us and put our minds at ease,' I say.

Chets backs up a few more steps, then stops. He takes his hand out of his pocket, hesitates for one, two breaths, and with a speed and grace I don't see coming, he pulls off his shoes and socks while running towards the far side of the Lookout, and throws them at us. I dodge a little too late and take a glancing blow to the side of my face. I feel the skin pull and tear. The other shoe finds its mark in Karim's eye socket, hitting him full force and knocking him to the ground. Kat runs to help him while I turn back to Chets. He takes a flying leap, getting maybe two metres of air, before landing high on the glass wall on both his hands and feet. Then he scuttles upwards, out of reach, and stares down at me.

'What the actual?' Mak shouts.

Trent scrabbles backwards across the floor, pizza still in hand, swearing like he's in a late-night Netflix B-movie.

There's a wet trickle sliding down my cheek, but I'll deal with that in a moment. I back up, my eyes never leaving Chets, until I'm level with the others, except Trent who is squashed right up against the wall furthest away from Chets.

'You OK, Karim?' I ask.

'Your friend is crawling up the walls like a woodlouse,' he says. 'And of all the things that could have happened to damage my gorgeous face in a horror-movie situation, I never would have guessed it would be being hit by a shoe.'

'Serves you right for calling me a slipper,' Chets shouts from his upside-down position just underneath the viewing platform.

'I guess he lied about having a plastic tree,' I say.

'You know my human mother always tries to keep up to date with the newest and most popular material items,' Chets calls. 'She wasn't about to display a plastic tree when the neighbours in the big houses were all getting Crater Lake cone trees. She bought the biggest one she could fit in the living room.'

'He's right,' I sigh. 'I should have known that. I let myself down there.'

'Lance, you're bleeding,' Ade says, grabbing a bunch of napkins from the floor and pressing them onto my face. 'Hold these here with as much pressure as you can.' I do as she says, cos even though I'm not that bothered about a little cut, we all know you don't argue with Ade.

'This is messed up,' Mak says. 'What the hell are we going to do now?'

20
The Sting

I try to think. First things first – we have to deal with Chets.

'Remember that everything we say or do will go back to the hive mind,' I say. 'So if you have any thoughts, keep them to yourself for now.'

'No, please say them out loud,' Chets says. 'We love seeing your little minds trying desperately to understand things that are million times bigger than you are.' And he says it in such a nasty way that I feel my temper raging, and I have to keep reminding myself that he isn't Chets. It's not really Chets talking, and it's not really Chets skulking up by the ceiling.

'We've been learning so much from you.' Chets does the creepy head tilt. 'It's extremely interesting to observe you figuring things out, and making your incredibly flawed plans, and all the while arguing and joking like the primitive creatures you are.'

'It's interesting to watch you scampering around on your bristly feet like a fly,' I say. 'And at least now I know how you got so good at gaming. I guess the physical changes started early with you, like they did with my mum. There's no way you'd be better than me without your spooky bug powers.'

'Our race is infinitely superior to yours. It's a miracle that you temporarily overcame us at Crater Lake. But we have been learning and changing, and this time you will not stop us.'

I want to be confident that we will, but at this moment I can't see how. We're trapped in the Lookout with alien Chets, and the rest of the swarm will be on their way here as soon as it's dark and they can move through town without drawing attention. We could try to make a break for it now, but there's no way we'd all make it out. Chets is too fast and too strong, and I have no doubt that he has other tricks up his sleeve. I'm not ready to sacrifice one of the group. I need to play this right.

'I hate to say I told you so,' Ade says. 'But I told you so. Chets was stalling the whole time – encouraging us to argue and dragging everything out so that we'd be stuck here when his re-inforcements arrived.'

'Right,' I say. 'But they're not here yet. There's one of him and five of us.'

Chets laughs. 'I knew you were a failure at maths, but I thought at least that you could count to six, which is how many there are of you, not that it will make a difference.'

'Oh, I wasn't counting Trent,' I say. 'I mean, let's face it, he's not going to help.'

'I seem to remember that I took out Chets at Crater Lake when he was chasing, and almost catching you,' Trent says.

'That was an accident,' I say. 'You were trying to save yourself.'

'And you wouldn't know your loser friend was a wall-crawler if it wasn't for me.'

'Also an accident,' Kat says.

'My point is that he can't stop all of us if we try to leave,' I say. 'Can you, Chets?'

He laughs in a very un-Chets-like way. 'You have no idea what we're capable of.'

And I don't. Which is why I'm trying to find out. 'Seen it all before, mate,' I say.

'But you haven't. You have only seen our first

incarnation. Now we are stronger in every way, and resolved to our purpose. At all costs.' He opens his mouth, stretching it wider and impossibly wider, his lips peeling back until there's a gaping black hole where his mouth was.

'I'd forgotten how gross this is,' Kat says, all of us staring transfixed by the horror.

'Is he eating his own head?' Karim whispers.

From the dark inside Chet's mouth, I see movement. Something is twitching around in there. Then shiny black structures, like thick insect legs, emerge from Chets' mouth – one on each side. They grow to about twenty, maybe twenty-five centimetres long, and the hooked ends clack together like pincers.

'Mandibles,' Ade says. 'They look different from last time.'

'They're thicker and hookier,' says Kat.

'Sharper edged, too. Look like they could take your arm off.' Mak edges a tiny bit closer to get a better look, and Chets snaps the mandibles at him in a way that suggests he'd happily give the arm chopping a go. Then he makes the noise – the noise that we refer to as 'The Hoche'.

'Take cover!' Mak yells, jumping over the coffee

table and flipping it onto its side in one smooth motion. It crosses my mind that I should probably work out more, cos he and Chets are totally shaming me, but then I move, pushing Kat and Karim towards the coffee table. 'Ade, the chair!' Mak shouts. She's the furthest away from the table, and as Chets' pincers spread wide and a ball of yellow slimy stuff shoots out from in between them, I can see she won't reach the shelter of the table. She freezes for half a second, then overturns the chair she was sitting on and dives behind it just in time.

The spit ball splats on the underside of the chair, and as I hit the deck behind the coffee table, I can literally hear it sizzling.

'You OK, Ade?' I call.

'Gucci,' her voice calls back.

'Sit tight for now, and holler if you need anything,' I say. I could really use her help right now, but if I talk loud enough for her to hear me, Chets will too. God, I miss texting.

She sighs, but I know she understands. 'OK. Shout me when you're ready.'

So I'm crouching behind a coffee table with Karim, Kat and Mak. Trent is just behind us, holding a cushion over his head like an umbrella, and trying to squash in between us so that he has the safest spot. The bonus of being behind the coffee table is that Chets can't see us, so if we're careful we can whisper without being heard.

'Any ideas, Mak?' I say.

He nods. 'Under the rug, there's a hatch to the bunker. If we can get down there, we'll have everything we need and it's totally bug proof.'

'Won't we be stuck down there, though?' I say.

He shakes his head. 'Secret exit.'

'Perfect.'

'If it's bug proof and has everything you need, why would you want to get out?' Trent says in his 'whispering' voice which is more like a bellowing cow. None of us even bother to shush him because there's honestly no point. I peek around the side of the table to see that Chets hasn't moved from his prime spot between the door and the entrance to the Tail. He hacks out another spit ball that I only just avoid. It flies past the place where my face was and splatters onto the floor.

'We'd better move fast,' I say. 'I'll distract Chets while you get the hatch open, Mak. Kat should climb down first cos she's fastest. Karim, you grab Ade and get yourselves down.'

'Can't I distract Chets and you get Ade?' Karim says, glancing across at the chair. 'I have an idea.'

'Chets is dangerous,' I say, cos I don't want Karim to risk himself. I feel like I dragged him into this situation and I'd never forgive myself if something happened to him.

'So is Ade,' Karim grimaces. 'Trust me, Lance. I can do this. You help Mak with the hatch.'

One of the most important things I learnt at Crater Lake is that you have to let people make their own choices. Everyone deserves a chance to be brave and to contribute, and if you allow people that chance, they'll most likely exceed expectations. It's about respect and trust.

'Alright,' I say. 'But be careful – he's a sharp shooter with those spit balls.'

'Understood. I've got this.' He unzips his pouch and pulls out a mini can of hairspray, and grabs Trent's cushion. 'Ready when you are.'

'OK, me and Kat will grab the rug and cover Mak while he opens the hatch. We won't have long. On three. One, two, three…'

Karim leaps out from behind the coffee table, using the cushion as a shield, and holds up the can of hairspray, pointing it towards Chets. 'You know what this is?' he says, side-stepping across the Lookout, past Ade's chair, moving towards the Tail.

As Chets turns to look at him, Kat and I jump the table and skid to the rug. She takes the nearest corner on the left, while I grab the right, and we lift it so that it forms a barricade between us and Chets. Mak slides over to the small trapdoor that was hidden underneath and pulls open an access panel next to it.

I watch Chets and Karim over the top of the rug. Karim has sidestepped back in our direction so that he's between us and Chets, but Chets is scuttling forward in short jerky bursts. He makes that hideous gurgling sound, and Karim squirts a short burst of hairspray at him. Chets jumps back slightly, and shoots a blob of goo at Karim, who blocks it with his cushion. Chets presses forward again. He's quick, and his movements are unpredictable. 'Nearly there, Mak?' I say.

'Two minutes.' He punches a code into a keypad. A green light flashes, then he enters another code.

'Ade!' I shout, 'You need to get over here.'

Ade launches towards us from behind the chair.

'Watch out!' Kat shouts, leaping at Ade and shoving her to the ground as a yellow ball narrowly misses hitting her right in the chest.

'He has double balls!' Karim shouts. 'He can shoot in two different directions.'

Kat and Ade are exposed, trying to pick themselves off the floor. Karim is taking a barrage of toxic spit. I have to draw some of the fire. 'Take the rug,' I shout to Mak, and I dart out into the middle of the room. As plans go, this one is failing horribly. A spit ball flies towards me, and I dodge it. I'm no ninja, but gaming has made my reflexes pretty sharp. I just have to stay alert. I dive for the tray that had our snacks on and snatch it up, sending glasses smashing and cheese puffs rolling. I lift it just in time to hear a gob of slime thunk onto it. Chets is holding the area between the two exits, but he's clearly suspicious of what's going on behind the rug, because he's pelting out spit balls and edging forwards. While Chets is looking at me, Karim darts forward with the hairspray and blasts some into Chets' face. Chets screeches and backs up a couple of metres.

'I reckon we can take him down,' Karim shouts. 'And get out of the door.'

And maybe we could. It's seriously risky, but I think it's worth taking the opportunity. We have a better chance of escape if half of us go out the door and half of us down the hatch. It'll be quicker, and there will be less chance of someone getting hit or left behind. 'Karim, join up,' I shout, and we move towards each other until we're side by side, with the protection of the cushion and the tray. Chets is still pawing at his eyes, and I reckon we can rush him. 'On three,' I say. 'One, two...' But I don't make it to three. I have eyes on Chets and I'm not liking what I'm seeing. He's started to shake, really hard.

'What's he doing?' Karim says.

'I don't know. This is new. Guys!' I call, and I glance over my shoulder at the others. The looks on their faces reflect how I'm feeling right now. Scared and disgusted, but also intrigued. We watch as Chets shudders, like when you disturb a cocoon and it goes nuts and you think it's going to explode caterpillar entrails all over you or something.

There's a ripping sound, and I can't make out what it is exactly – clothes, or skin, or something else. Chets turns, so that his head is closest to the wall, and his feet towards us, then he peels his feet from the ceiling and slowly lowers himself down so that he's vertical – his hands still stuck on the ceiling and holding all of his bodyweight like it's nothing. He's not just dangling there, though, his knees are bent up towards his stomach, like he's halfway through a pull-up. It's like he's poised. Ready.

And then something starts extending down from Chets' butt area that makes the mandibles look tame. It's black and covered in vicious-looking hooks, about ten centimetres thick at the base and tapering in a curve to a knifepoint at the tip. Imagine Wolverine having one large black claw, coming out of his lower back rather than his knuckles. It's the nastiest looking thing I've ever seen.

'A stinger,' I say, unable to tear my eyes away from it. 'He's got a stinger.'

21
Truth

Karim grabs my arm and we take a step back, our eyes fixed on the nastiness in front of us. 'It's covered in tiny thorns,' he says. 'That's gotta hurt coming out. Worse than a peanut poo.' I don't speak, I just watch transfixed as Chets uses his hand to pull himself forward across the ceiling, his back curled so that his butt tilts forwards, the stinger pointed at us.

Then the spell is broken when I hear what I can only describe as a roar from Mak. I risk a glance over my shoulder just in time to see Trent disappearing down the hatch and closing it behind him.

'Son of a...' Mak flings himself on it and tries the keypad. The light flashes red. 'He's locked himself in.'

'Abort!' I shout. 'Back to the table.'

The girls are up now and holding the rug over

Mak while he has one last try at getting the hatch open. Karim and I back up and make for the shelter of the rug, too. Chets obviously knows he's won, so he walks on his hands back to his spot, happy to keep us in the annex until the rest of the swarm arrives to put us to sleep. We pull the rug over the legs of the table so we have a sort of ceiling and a bit more protection, then we sit and try to catch our breath.

'Chets grew a stinger,' Kat says. 'A massive, spiky stinger.'

'He did warn us that they've evolved. I guess that means being able to launch multiple spit balls, and unleash a beast of a stinger.' I massage my forehead and close my eyes for a second. 'They were dangerous at Crater Lake, but that seems like nothing compared to this. I don't think he'll take us on by himself in case one of us gets out – he just wants to keep us here until reinforcements arrive. Still, we'd better keep eyes on Chets at all times.'

'I'll take first watch,' Kat says, shuffling to the edge of the table and peering around it. 'I want another look anyway.'

'I wonder what the stinger does, exactly,' Ade says.

'Apart from sting?' Karim says.

Ade looks at him less aggressively than she was an hour ago. 'There are different kinds of stings, though. Some hurt, some paralyse, and some kill.'

'I hadn't thought of that.' I suddenly feel dead tired. 'Do you think it releases the same stuff that makes up the sedative spit balls?'

'I mean, it might,' Ade says.

'But...' Karim looks about as worried as I feel.

Ade starts pulling clips out of her hair and putting them in a pile on the floor. 'But it wouldn't make sense from an evolutionary point of view. They already have the sedative spit; whatever toxin is in the stinger is probably something different.'

'And by something different, you mean something worse?' I ask, cos let's face it, that's the important question right now, and as much as part of me doesn't want to hear the answer, we need to plan around the worst-case scenario.

Ade unwinds her hair from a spongy doughnut thing that was on top of her head. 'I expect so.' She puts the doughnut on the ground next to the pile of clips and rubs the part of her head where her hair dollop was a moment ago. 'God, that's such a relief – it was giving me the worst headache.'

'I have a spare scrunchie if you want one?' Kat says, taking a band off her wrist and passing it to Ade.

'Thanks, Kat,' Ade smiles, and I know she's not just saying thank you for the hairband.

'I'm gonna kill Trent.' Mak is fuming. 'What a snake.'

'Yeah,' I sigh. 'It's not the best. What's Chets doing, Kat?'

'He's put his pincers and stinger away. He's back in his original position and it looks like he's trying to clean his face. That was a good idea, with the hairspray.'

'Never leave home without it,' Karim grins.

'So my plan was a disaster,' I say. 'And now we're stuck and it's my fault. Sorry, guys – this is the worst.'

'It wasn't your fault,' Ade says. 'We had no way of knowing that Chets had evolved new weaponry.'

'I'm gonna kill him,' Mak says again. 'We should never have let him in.'

'If we hadn't let him in, we wouldn't have found out about Chets,' I say. 'And we'd be sitting here not knowing that the swarm is about to attack us.'

'This might sound weird,' Kat says. 'But I actually found it quite reassuring when Trent jumped down the hatch. Everything has changed so much the last few months – it's kind of nice that some things are the same. Chets is an alien wasp, and Trent left us all in the poop to save himself. It's like old times.'

'You know, most people's old times are like rounders in the park, or eating marshmallows round a campfire.' Karim puts his hairspray back in his pouch.

'How long till it gets dark?' I say, just as the first chimes ring out from St Anthony's. My heart sinks. 'We're running out of time. What are we going to do?'

'We'll think of something,' Kat says. 'Don't lose hope, Lance. We're all here together, and that's something I would have said was impossible if you'd asked me yesterday.'

'Same,' says Ade.

'Yeah,' Mak nods. 'How did we let things get so bad between us?'

'Well, from what I can tell, it started when you met Georgia-Rae and totally disappeared up her Huaraches,' Karim says. 'And that seems to have snapped something that was already pulled too tight in Adrianne, possibly from the transition to high school.'

We all look at Karim.

'Just saying,' he says. 'No offence.'

'The new boy is right,' Chets calls over. 'And the situation was exacerbated by the falling out between Adrianne and Katja.'

'You should have come to Bing with me.' Trent's voice rings out across the Lookout, making me jump. 'I would have looked after you.'

'Great, he's found the intercom,' Mak sighs.

'I don't need looking after,' Ade snaps. 'Stay out of this, Trent. You lost your right to an opinion when you locked us out of the bunker.'

'It is sick down here,' Trent says. 'I can stay in this bunker for however long it takes you lot to sort out the alien stuff.'

'We could have all gone down there,' I say.

'If you were down here, you wouldn't be dealing with the situation up there. Also, I didn't want to risk Chetan stinging me. However, I am willing to consider a deal.'

'What kind of deal?' Kat asks.

'I will allow Adrianne, and only Adrianne, to

enter the bunker if she brings down a couple of bottles of coke. I can only find water down here, and weird milk powder. Then we can sit this out together.'

'I'd honestly rather become a host to a vile alien parasite,' Ade says.

'And we need her,' I say. She smiles.

'What happened, Ade?' Kat says. 'I mean, you don't have to talk about it if you don't want to, but I really want to understand.'

Ade looks at Kat, then down at her doughnut and clips on the floor. 'It was loads of things. Back in primary I always felt so sure of myself. I knew what I liked, and who I liked, and I knew what I wanted. I never really had any doubts about anything. Then we got to Latham and all the rules changed. There were loads of smart, confident people like me, and I know this sounds awful, but I was so used to being head girl – the only head girl. It threw me a bit that there were other head girls in every class.'

I've never been the best at anything, so I don't really know how it feels to suddenly face competition where there was none before. But it was hard at first having hundreds of kids in our year group when there used to be just thirty. So many new people, and everyone trying to be top dog. My way of dealing was to go back to my old ways, sitting in the back of the class, mucking around and having a laugh. Ade obviously chose a different way to deal.

'And there was this new thing that had never been an issue before.' Her cheeks are pink and she's scraping at the floor with one of the hair clips. 'All anyone talked about was who was fit and who wasn't. I mean – it's pathetic. I know that people's worth has nothing to do with what they look like. But for some reason, it bothered me. For the first time in my life, I felt embarrassed about what I look like – that I'm not pretty.' She sucks in her cheeks, and I can see how hard it is for her to say this stuff. 'I got so angry, with everyone else for thinking that being fit has any value. With Kat because she's beautiful and couldn't understand what I was feeling. With Mak, because he went off with Georgia-Rae. And so, so angry with myself for caring about any of it.' She looks up. 'Honestly, I hate that it bothers me. I hate it, but I can't seem to switch it off.' She brushes a tear off her cheek, but another one quickly follows. And I don't know what to say.

'I'm so sorry, Ade.' Kat puts an arm around her. 'I never realised. I hated that you were changing yourself and I never stopped to wonder why. I should have been supporting you and listening to you, but instead I gave you such a hard time. I thought you were just being an idiot. I wish you'd told me.'

'I couldn't,' Ade says. 'So I got mad at you.'

'And that's how you two fell out?' Karim says. 'Wow. Girls are complicated.'

'And I know it doesn't matter,' Kat says, looking like she's going to cry too. 'But how can you think you're not pretty?'

'Yeah,' Mak says. 'How can you think that? Not that it matters.'

Karim and I look at each other, and I can tell he's as alarmed as I am by where this conversation is heading.

'Yeah,' Trent says. 'You are fine, girl.'

And we all crack up laughing, cos Trent is the worst and Kat's right – it's kind of nice that some things don't change.

'Ade,' Kat says. 'Of all the people I have ever met, there is no one I'd rather be more like than you.'

'Same,' I say.

'For sure,' Mak nods.

'I've only known you for one day, so I'm going to wait and decide later, if that's OK?' Karim says, and we all laugh again.

'Pathetic humans,' Chets says from the ceiling. 'You are all inferior.' And that just makes us laugh harder.

'I guess I should say something, too,' Mak says, when we've calmed down a bit. He bites his lip. 'Georgia-Rae dumped me.'

'Oh, Maksym,' Kat says. 'I'm sorry. What happened?'

'I honestly don't really know,' he says. 'Like, with any of it. We met in tutorial on the first week and had some of the same classes, so we started walking together. Then we were meeting in the park after school, and then it was kind of like when you're two thirds of the way through a sharing bucket. You know if you keep going, it will make you feel sick, but you've gone too far to stop or turn back. You're going to finish that bucket whatever.'

'At what point did you decide it was a good idea to get your ear pierced?' I ask.

'Oh man, I hate it. But she wanted us to get matching earrings.'

'You know you could have said no,' I say, trying not to laugh.

'I totally lost it,' Mak says. 'It was like I turned into a different person. We even did a Christmas snow-globe photo together.'

'Do you have it?' Karim says. 'Please say you have it.'

'I'm not showing you.' Mak shoves his hands in his pockets.

'But you'll feel better about it once it's out in the open,' Kat says. 'And it would really cheer Ade up. Wouldn't it, Ade?'

Ade sniffs. 'Yes, I think it would help a lot.'

Mak sighs and pulls his phone out of his pocket, then scrolls for a bit. 'Here.' He holds the phone up to show us a picture of him and Georgia-Rae kneeling inside the snow-globe looking into each other's eyes, throwing the fake snow up into the air, and doing these huge open-mouthed fake smiles. I mean, we all have a million pics of ourselves, with stupid filters that make us look a hundred years old, or totally deformed, or with our faces swapped. And they're funny. But this is probably the cringiest photo I have ever seen.

'Are you wearing…' I say.

'Matching Christmas jumpers? Yes.' He sighs again.

'And this cost you how much?' Karim asks.

'Twelve ninety-nine for the photos, then another tenner so that Georgia-Rae could have one put inside a miniature snow-globe to keep in her bedroom. And…' he hesitates.

'You might as well get it off your chest, Mak,' I say.

Kat nods. 'Rip off the plaster.'

Mak sighs again. 'I also spent fifteen pounds to have the picture on a cushion.'

'To cuddle?' Karim says.

Mak puts his hands over his face and nods, and it's all I can do to keep the laugh from exploding out of my face.

'Is that what you hid under the duvet when you were showing us around?' Ade asks. 'A cushion with yours and Georgia-Rae's faces on it, pretending to play in some plastic snow?'

'I think I'd use the word "frolic",' Karim says. 'I've never said it before in my life, but it feels right.'

'Sounds like something little lambs do in fields of daisies,' I say.

Adrianne pulls Mak's phone closer to her face for a better look. 'I think frolic works.'

'Will somebody please hold this picture up so I can see?' Chets calls from his corner.

'I want to see, too,' Trent's voice blasts through the intercom.

Mak shrugs and lifts the phone above the table so Chets can see.

'Definitely frolicking,' Chets says. And that's it, we all totally lose it, even Mak. I laugh so hard that I can't breathe. I laugh so hard that it really, really hurts. And I look at the others rolling around and holding their bellies, and it makes me laugh even harder. We keep going for about five minutes, until we ache, and tears are running down our faces, and then we finally pull ourselves together.

'Not fair, I want to see,' Trent whines. 'You guys suck.' And it sets us off all over again.

'Are you upset about breaking up?' Kat says, when she's able to speak again.

'I was at first. Well, for quite a while, really, but I was starting to see the positives. Like I used to have to message her all the time, and if I didn't like her posts within ten minutes of her putting them up, she got mad at me. So it was nice not having to deal with that. Also, we didn't really have anything in common. She wanted me to be supportive of her interests, so I had to do her stuff all the time, which was mostly making TikToks and watching shows about drag queens. I mean, they were alright, but I would have liked to have watched something different once in a while. So before you turned up, I was starting to realise that I was actually a bit relieved about it all, and it made me see things differently. Now that I think about it, I'm not sure she even liked me that much. She was annoyed with me, like, eighty per cent of the time.'

'Oh Mak.' Kat rubs his arm. 'I'm glad you're OK.'

'It's not your fault,' he says. 'I wanted to let you all know, but after totally breaking bro code and ditching you all for months, I was scared.'

'We would have been here like a shot, man,' I say.

'I know. And I'm glad you're here now, even though we're trapped by alien Chets.'

'This Georgia-Rae.' Trent's voice rings out again. 'Can I have her number?'

We all groan.

'Anyone else want to share something with the group?' Karim says. 'Cos I feel like we're really bonding.'

'Can I ask a question?' Mak says. 'Why do you carry a man pouch everywhere? The word at school is that you're carrying something you shouldn't be, but now I'm thinking it's full of styling products.'

'Nah, that's just a nice little extra,' Karim says. 'I'm diabetic, so I have to keep snacks, my blood-sugar testing kit and an epi-pen with me at all times. Plus, the pouch makes me look cool – it's like the Karim trademark accessory.'

'So that's why you and Lance hang out together – you're both freaks with weird diseases,' Trent snorts.

'Is there any way of turning the intercom off?' Kat asks.

'Not from up here, unfortunately.' Mak clenches a fist. 'I'm honestly going to kill him.'

'FYI, Lance and I hang out together because we're both incredibly cool, funny and good-looking,' Karim shouts into the air. 'And my mum always says that my diabetes is my superpower.'

'Like Lance's sleep apnoea is his,' Kat grins. 'We would never have survived Crater Lake without his ability to be amazing, even when he's had no sleep.'

'My CPAP helped, too,' I say. And just the thought of it makes me realise how tired I am. I look around at the others. Karim is pale, Kat looks exhausted, and Ade and Mak don't look great either. They might have got more sleep than we did last night, but it's been a long day, and the stuff with Chets and Trent has left its mark. Part of me wishes I'd brought my portable CPAP with me, so we could get some rest, but with the hive knowing where we are and it starting to get dark, we wouldn't be able to close our eyes anyway. We're not sleeping until this is over.

'How are we gonna finish this?' I ask, lowering my voice again so that Chets won't hear, and hopefully Trent won't either. 'Even if only a quarter of the people in Straybridge have been turned into sporelings, that's still way more than we can tardigrade back.'

'We could lure them to one of the rivers,' Kat

says. 'But they're not exactly deep or fast. They'd just be able to wade across and climb out.'

'And there's no dam to destroy to create a rush of water like we had in the crater, so I don't know how we'd get them all in,' says Mak.

Karim has taken over Chets-watch, so he whispers through the side of his mouth. 'But if we don't fix things by the end of today, it's game over. The cones are going to open tomorrow and release millions of spores, and everyone in town will go buggy, even if they don't have a tree in their house. I really don't want to be a sporeling, guys. Stingers should not be growing out of human butts – it just isn't right.'

'OK, so we can't take out all of them,' I say, trying to connect my thoughts, like a map. 'But the difference with them this time is that their physical and mental qualities seem to be separate. My mum was well and strong in her body, but she didn't go creepy until the XGen was turned off. So if we can turn it back on, we might be able to press pause on the hive mind.'

Ade nods. 'It won't get rid of the spores, but it will give us time to find a long-term solution.'

'So we've got to get back to the university,'

Karim groans. 'Even though it's heavily guarded and full of horrifying things.'

'And that disgusting pukey smell,' says Kat.

Mak peers around the table. 'We can get out through the Lookout door, or the concealed exit in the Tail, but how are we going to get past Chets?'

'I've been thinking about that,' I say. 'And I don't think we can all get past him, but if I keep him busy, the rest of you can get out.' And I'm not surprised when they all look mad and say 'no way' at the same time. 'Someone's got to stay behind, and it's going to be me.'

'Why should it automatically be you?' Ade asks.

'Yeah, we should at least Geek, Robot, Overlord for it,' says Mak.

'Because we need Ade's speed and smarts, Kat's climbing skills, Mak's survival info and strength, and Karim's knowledge of the university and XGen. I'm the least useful in this situation.' And I'm not saying it for sympathy, or to come across like the tragic hero. It's fact.

'Na-ah,' Kat says. 'We can't do it without you. You work out all the tactics.'

'And you think the most clearly under pressure,' says Ade.

'Plus, you're a ballsy son of a gun.' Karim whacks me on the shoulder.

'Every group of survivors needs a leader,' says Mak. 'And you're ours.'

'You are our greatest treasure, and must be protected at all costs,' Karim says.

'That's it,' I say. 'That's what it means! The bug-eyes have a leader who they will protect at all costs. Their Sith Master. Their Palpatine. Keeping their queen alive will come before anything and everything else.' I grin. 'I know how we're getting out of here.'

22
The Swarm

I go through the plan as quickly and quietly as I can. We need everyone on board if it's going to work, but I don't even need to question whether they're with me or not, because they always, always have my back. Of course it's risky as hell, but we're running out of time and options, and sometimes risky is necessary.

Step one is the worst part – waiting. We need as many of the Straybridge sporelings as possible to be here at the annex and thinking that we've given up and are planning to stay holed up. Waiting for something scary is always worse than the scary thing itself, cos once it happens you can deal with it. While you're waiting, there's nothing you can really do, so the scary thing builds in your mind until it seems impossible to overcome. Keeping a lid on your fear – that's the hardest part.

We lower the shutters to the annex so we can't

see what's going on outside, and we use the time to talk, and to laugh, throwing out a few bits of false information every now and then, to throw Chets (and Trent) off the scent.

The noises outside start just before the final curfew bells ring out. There's a slight rattling of the shutters as though they're being pushed and pulled to test for weaknesses.

'They'll hold for a while.' Mak sounds reassuringly unworried. 'They were made to withstand intruders.'

'Even super-strong ones?' Kat says.

'Don't worry. They'll keep us safe for long enough.'

'Long enough for what?' Chets says. 'Do you think someone is coming to rescue you? Straybridge is cut off from the rest of the world. Nobody knows what's happening here. No help is coming.'

'You don't know everything, Chets,' I say.

'I have the wisdom of the hive mind. I know more than you.'

'We'll see.'

'They're on the roof,' Ade says as the peeling Velcro sound rips across the ceiling high above us.

We sit and listen, as the scratching and dragging of sporeling hands and feet grows around us, and a few bristled palms become several, and then loads. We can't see through the metal shutters, and I wonder if my mum is out there among the bugs.

'How many do you think?' Karim says.

'More than thirty,' Mak says with absolute certainty. 'I'd say up to fifty.'

'A swarm,' Ade says.

'It's time,' I nod. 'Ready?'

'Always,' Mak says.

'Born ready,' Kat smiles.

'Wait,' Ade says. 'Just a second.' She turns to Mak. 'I think it's time we lost the earrings. Let's face it, mine mean I'm more likely to get my ear lobes ripped off, and yours just looks ridiculous.'

Mak laughs. 'I will if you will.'

Kat gasps and grabs my arm. 'This is such a moment, guys.'

Ade pulls out her giant gold hoops and hands them to Kat. 'You can have the honour of throwing them away.'

Mak removes his bling and flicks it across the room, and then they sit grinning at each other, like the earring removal was symbolic of something else, and I'm not sure where it's going but I'm so freaking happy that we're all friends again.

'I'm sorry, but I need to selfie this moment,' Kat says, taking her phone out of her pocket. She doesn't say 'just in case' but I feel like it's there, hovering in the air between all of us. I imagine a handful of human rebel fighters finding her phone, years in the future, and realising that this was the last selfie taken before the world ended and the human race faced total annihilation. But then I realise I'm being a drama queen, so I huddle in and pull my best stupid selfie pose.

'If I angle it right, I can even get Chets in the background,' Kat says. 'Everybody say "certain death!"' We all crack up, and then look at the photo and laugh even harder at Chets' peed-off face in the corner.

'Right, let's do it,' I say. 'Unless Karim wants to take off his dodgy gold chain first, and add it to the reject pile.'

'Hey, this was a gift,' Karim says.

I stand up, and the others stand next to me, with the sound of claws scraping metal all around us, and my body-snatched best friend Hoching up in the corner of the ceiling.

Mak points at a spot on the wall behind the viewing platform, next to where the Lookout leads into the Tail. 'That's the fake wall,' he says in a low voice. 'If you hit it at around chest level and slightly to the left, it shouldn't blow up.'

'You never said it could blow up!' Kat squeaks. 'What have you got in there?'

'Probably best you don't know,' Mak says.

Kat sprints over to the steep stairs that lead to the viewing platform, and starts to climb, at the same time that Karim takes a step towards Chets with his epi-pen held up, and I move forwards with the hairspray.

'Flank him,' I say.

Chets is still growing his mandibles, so he's not quite ready to fire yet.

'Did you put the tardigrades into the syringe?' I ask Karim.

'This baby is fully tardigrade loaded,' he says. I think he thinks he's in an action movie. We move to either side of Chets, who turns his head from me to Karim and back again, his mandibles almost fully extended now. In a moment he'll be ready to spit.

'I know you can't talk right now, Chets,' I say.

'So you should just listen. We have PVPs and an epi-pen full of tardigrades. If we inject you, you'll be human again in seconds.'

He releases his feet from the ceiling and gets into stinger mode, the black claw-like spear emerging from his lower back. Now that I'm closer to it, I can see a drop of clear liquid sitting right on the tip. Ade was right, it looks different from the sedative spit and, for half a second, I think this plan was a terrible idea. He tilts his head towards me, then Karim, and scuttles forward a couple of steps.

In the corner of my eye, I can see that Kat is in place. It's now or never.

'The funny thing is,' I say, 'that this has just been a distraction. What you really should have been worried about is Kat opening the trapdoor to the ceiling and tardigrading the rest of the swarm.'

Chets' head flicks toward Kat, and then he moves. He flips his feet back onto the ceiling, and then on all fours, and I'm not even exaggerating here, he gallops like a freaking backwards horse towards Kat, stinger pointed right at her.

She was standing on the platform, but she

somehow finds finger grips on the wall and climbs higher, without looking behind her. In two seconds, she's at the spot Mak pointed out and, honestly, I could never have got up there in two hours. Chets charges towards her, and it looks like she hasn't seen him coming. I call out a warning, at the exact same time the others do, but I shouldn't have worried. At the very last moment, she jumps to the side, above the entrance to the Tail, clinging on with her fingertips and toes, and Chets crashes into the spot she held a second before, stinger first, piercing the hollow wall.

I hold my breath, hoping so hard that it's worked, and that it will give us the time to do what we need to do. Chets shrieks and makes to follow Kat – his hands pacing quickly forwards. But then he jerks back again as his feet can't follow. His stinger is wedged into the fake wall. He can't move.

Karim leaps for the shutter controls, as Kat climbs down to the Tail, and runs in with Mak and Ade behind her. He hits the button to lift the shutters at the same time that Kat pings the microwave on in the kitchen.

Chets freezes, stuck in the wall, and now in a

glitch. Hopefully he can't communicate with the hive mind. The microwave glitch doesn't extend to the sporelings outside, who are curling their fingers under the rising shutters, trying to get them up more quickly. Karim and I stand close to the glass, as the shutters move upwards, making us visible to the swarm outside, and revealing the horror surrounding us. In ten seconds, we're looking out at the horde of wasp people, who all seem desperate to get to us and do god knows what. It's horrible. At Crater Lake the sporelings all had the weird eyes, which I'd been looking for on Mum but didn't spot. Now that it's dark, I see they all have glowing yellow rings around their pupils. It's a clever adaptation – makes them undetectable during the day but gives them the night vision when they need it. Then I see Mum snarling, her mandibles out, and I look away, focussing on the others. If we get through this, I'll have to sit across the table from her and I don't want to be picturing pincers.

'Look, there's Shrina from tutor group,' Karim says, giving her a little wave. She snaps her pincers at him. 'I'm taking that as a wave back.'

I gaze around at a sea of familiar faces, now all

distorted with lips peeled back and mandibles snapping. The guy with the long hair who works in the game shop is in there. I bought a new controller from him last weekend. The Business Studies teacher from Latham, whose name I can't remember, is trying to pry open the door. A kid I recognise from Montmorency Primary, maybe three years below us, is trying to smash the glass wall. I think his name is Henry. There's also Mrs McAllister, one of our neighbours, hanging upside down from the roof, hitting the window with a bit of pipe. She's like the oldest person I've ever seen, and it looks a whole world of wrong. Mak and Kat join us at the glass.

'Woah,' Kat says. 'This is like a nightmare.'

'Yeah.' I watch the bugs all clamouring to get into the Lookout, clambering over each other and up the walls, and if this is the way the world ends, it's genuinely horrific. If we survive this, I know I'll be replaying this scene in my mind for the rest of my life. I feel a wave of tiredness pulling me down, making me want to curl up on the floor and close my eyes. Then I look across at my friends and see that they're all struggling, too.

'Did Ade make it out?' I say.

'Off like a rocket,' Mak smiles.

And knowing that Ade is out there, putting herself in danger, and pushing herself so that she can help all of us gives me that kick I need to step up.

'Do you think she'll make it?' Karim asks.

'It's Ade,' I say. 'She's crazy fast and crazy smart. She'll make it.'

'I just hope the Lookout holds out for long enough,' Mak says, as a sporeling hurls a rock at one of the walls and the crash makes us all jump. More rocks are thrown, thunking onto the glass like an apocalyptic hail storm.

'Ten minutes, that's all she needs to get to the university, and then another couple of minutes to set off the alarm.' I watch as a group of bugs run at the door with a tree trunk.

'I wish she wasn't alone.' Kat sniffs, as the door shudders.

'Me too. But it was the best way. And with almost all of the sporelings here, she has a good chance of getting there without running into trouble.'

'I'm gonna get the stuff together – radios, tardigrades, firelighters and some light weapons in case we do have to fight our way out of here,' Mak says. And I know it's a good idea, but the thought of fighting these people who used to be our family, friends and neighbours makes me feel sick.

'Good thinking,' I say. 'Grab anything you think might be helpful, and load up some backpacks.'

'What's happening up there?' Trent's voice booms. 'What's all the banging?'

'It's about a hundred alien parasites,' Karim says. 'They've found the secret entrance to the bunker and they're coming for you.'

'They can't get in though, right?' Trent says. 'This place looks like it was built to survive a nuclear attack.'

'Not sure.' Mak comes back with four backpacks and a plate of brownies. 'It's never been tested, so it could go either way.' He offers us the brownies. 'These are special – since Crater Lake, Dad and Zuzie have been experimenting with their baking.'

Karim takes a massive bite. 'Is good,' he mumbles through his mouthful.

'And they have a bonus ingredient,' Mak grins, 'that should give us an extra layer of protection against the spores.'

'Are these tardibrownies?' Kat asks.

'Yep. Packed full of chocolate and water bears.'

The door shudders again, and there's an awful snapping noise from somewhere above us.

'Wait, are you saying I just swallowed a mouthful of those wrinkly hippo things?' Karim says, looking down at the rest of his brownie.

'Genius,' I say, taking a bite of mine.

'I feel a bit bad,' says Kat. 'Thank you for your sacrifice, guys,' she whispers to the brownie.

'I want a brownie!' Trent shouts.

'Will I be able to see them wriggling around in my poo, then?' Karim is still inspecting his brownie.

'They're too small,' I say. 'You can only see them with a microscope.'

'You could give them a little wave before you flush, though,' says Kat. 'Just in case they can see you.'

'And eating them will mean I won't turn into one of those?' Karim points at the swarm outside.

Mak goes in for a second brownie. 'I don't know for sure, but there's a good chance they'll prevent the spores from taking over your body.'

'Not fair, I want one,' Trent calls again, and by this point we don't even bother responding to him.

'And they don't die when you cook them?'

'They can withstand extremes of temperature,' I say. 'They can even survive in space.'

'Tardigrades.' Karim takes another bite of brownie. 'Who knew?'

I've been trying not to clock-watch, or keep working out where on her journey Ade will be, but it's hard. If she succeeds, and my theory is correct, we should know about it pretty much straight away. I don't want to think about what will happen if she doesn't make it.

A rock hits the panel of glass closest to me. It doesn't hit with as much force as some of the others have, so there's no loud thud, but it hits in a way that causes more damage. I hear a sharp cracking sound, and see a pea-sized crater in the glass.

'We'd better get ready,' Mak says. 'They have a weakness now. It won't take long to spread.'

So we swallow our brownies and pull on our backpacks, tightening the straps so that they fit securely against our bodies. We re-tie our shoelaces and Kat puts her hair in a ponytail. Karim does some lunges, which makes us all laugh. 'For the jogging,' he says. And then there's nothing to do but wait.

The bugs are concentrated around the damaged glass, hitting it with rocks, branches and their mandibles. Cracks start to splinter out from the hole. We back towards the entrance to the Tail – it has a shutter that we can close after us to buy us some more time. Chets is still frozen, his stinger wedged into the wall, his mandibles wide and his mouth open. I can hear the microwave churning on in the kitchen – something else that should keep the bugs at bay for a short while, until they find a way around it.

The bug that was Mrs McAllister has the point of her gnarly mandible inside the hole in the glass, working away at it, wrenching and pulling, with her hands and feet planted on the glass to give her purchase. I hear the crack as a chunk of glass finally gives way. It's like breaking the surface of a frozen puddle. A shard the size of my hand comes away, followed by another, even bigger piece.

The power to the Lookout cuts out, plunging us into darkness for a couple of seconds. Then Mak clicks on a battery-powered floodlight. It glows a dull orange, making everything look like the inside of a volcano. Not that I've been inside a volcano, but this is how I imagine it to look –

burnt orange and full of shadows. The power failure has shut down the microwave, and I can see Chets unglitching and trying to untrap himself from the hollow wall.

'This is it,' I say, as we huddle closer, facing the swarm. 'We got this.'

Mrs McAllister pushes her face through the hole, apparently not bothered about the sharp edges of the glass cutting her skin. She clacks her mandibles at us, as blood trickles down her cheek and spatters onto the floor of the Lookout.

'It's lucky that years of playing violent video-games has desensitised us to this kind of thing,' Karim says.

Her shoulders force some more glass loose. It smashes onto the floor and she gets an arm inside, using it to push back on the wall and propel herself forward.

Another pane of glass cracks from floor to ceiling, and the bugs clamber over each other, trying to break it down.

'I love you guys,' Kat says, as we back up closer to the Tail, ready to fall back so we can make one last stand. We have only seconds until they're on us.

It crosses my mind that my plan has failed. That I misjudged it all. That this really is the end. But I'm not giving up. Not yet. 'She'll make it,' I say out loud.

Mrs McAllister finally widens the hole enough that she can climb through, into the room. She flings herself forward in a movement that is half leap, half flight, releasing spit balls as she does. We block them with our cushion shields, but as a whole section of the glass wall on our right comes crashing down, I know we have to move.

'The Tail!' I say, as bugs swarm across the floor, up the walls and onto the ceiling, trying to block our retreat. They're pouring in now, spit balls flying, mandibles snapping. The sound of hoching is all around us and unbearably loud.

Then it stops. Every sporeling at the exact same moment freezes, mid-attack, and tilts their head, like they're listening. There's one, maybe two seconds of silence and stillness, then they turn and swarm out of the building through the holes they made. One after the other, like an army of ants pouring out of an anthill. They're fast, efficient, working as one, and then they're gone.

23
At All Costs

'Ade did it,' Mak says. 'Legend.'

'What did Ade do exactly?' Chets hisses. He's still struggling to free himself from the wall, wriggling and pulling, his face bright red.

'Bit of a design flaw to your stinger,' I say. 'You'll probably want to evolve that differently next time.'

'We're not done, yet,' Chets says. 'A threat to the queen is just that – a threat. The swarm will be there in minutes, and the threat will be neutralised, at all…'

'Costs. Yeah, we know. And, on that note,' I say. 'Shall we, guys?'

'Bye, Chets.' Kat waves at him. 'I hope you're less terrifying when I see you next.' She walks into the Tail.

'Take care, man,' says Mak. 'Maybe eat some brownies and chill for a bit.' He follows Kat through the doorway.

'Er, nice to meet you,' Karim says. 'Well not really, but anyway.' He jogs after Mak.

'Whatever you have planned, you'll fail,' Chets says, narrowing his chocolate eyes at me. 'The hive cannot lose.'

I take one last look at him, and the truth is that I really don't know how this is gonna go. But I do know that we have a chance, and sometimes that's all you need. 'We'll see. Bye, Chets.'

I run into the Tail and out of Chets' view. The last things I hear are him screeching and Trent shouting, 'Where's everyone going? Is it safe to come out?'

We leave the annex through the concealed exit at the back of the storage room, so that Chets can't see us, and bolt through the woods and into the fields, following the same route that Ade took earlier.

Straggler's Fields are wide and empty of people, lit by the moon and smelling of frost. After being enclosed in the annex, with every intake of breath filling my nose with the sickly scent of the sporelings, the fields are like medicine. The headache that had been thumping behind my eyes clears, and the clean air sweeps away the sick feeling that had been churning in my stomach. I enjoy the feel of the wind cutting blades against my face, and I forget to be tired as the muscles in my legs thrum with energy. We don't talk as we run – there's no need as we all know the plan. I wonder what the others are thinking, whether they're scared or excited, or maybe focussing on the random stuff that usually seems so important. We disturb a group of wild rabbits nibbling at the grass and send them bobbing into their burrow. I see bats flitting over the river, looking for insects, and hear a fox barking from the far bank. It's kind of reassuring that some things are going on like the apocalypse isn't happening. It's just the birds, or rather the fact that there aren't any, that makes things feel different. I wonder how they knew to fly away and where they've gone.

We follow the River Brink as we did the day before, but this time heading towards the university. We don't have to hide this time, as we know most of the bugs are busy, so we make good progress. Not as fast as Ade, obviously, but it isn't long before we're cutting through the golf course, sprinting under the big bridge, and dodging between the gravestones in the cemetery.

I signal to the others to stop as we see the masts of the Cake looming up ahead of us. They used to be lit up at night, but they're dead now – just ghostly white figures standing on the roof, looking out across the campus.

'So,' I say, knowing this might be the last time I talk to my friends. 'One last check that we have the right supplies.'

We each take off our backpacks, open them and rummage inside. When we split up, we'll need specific items to carry out our parts of the plan. I go to zip my bag up, but then take some of the contents out and stuff them in my socks.

'Radio silence, unless it's life or death,' I say. 'How long do you think you'll need to find the water source and get inside, Mak?'

'I'm pretty sure I know where it is, but accessing it might be tricky. Say ten minutes, give or take.'

'I'll let you two in the fire exit at the back, and then I can be on the roof in two.' Kat grins. 'I'll hide there until I hear from Karim.'

'Make sure you do,' I say. 'I don't think the standard bugs will be up there, but there's still...'

'Digger, I know. I'll be careful, promise.'

'I'll make sure Karim has a free run to his mum's office, then I'll try to locate Ade,' I say. 'She should be within radio distance once I'm inside.'

'And I'll get on Mum's computer and get XGen back on,' Karim says. 'You sure you know how to reboot the masts, Kat?'

'I'm sure,' Kat nods.

'How are you going to distract the bugs?' Karim says. 'There are a crud-ton of aliens in there, and only one of you.'

'I have a few ideas,' I say, not wanting to give them too much detail in case they try to stop me. 'But until I get there and see what the deal is, I can't say for sure what will work best. Lucky I can think on my feet.' I grin. 'The important thing is getting you in, Karim, and then you just have to work as fast as you can.'

'Understood.'

We look at each other for a couple of seconds, our breath coming out in white clouds and mingling together.

'Group hug moment?' Karim says, and we all groan, tighten our backpacks, and jog towards the back of the Cake.

The building is mostly dark, though individual

windows light up in sequence, one after the other, as though someone is moving methodically from room to room. There are a couple of bug security guards patrolling the outside. They walk the perimeter of the building, stopping every ten metres or so to look out across the campus, the yellow rings in their eyes standing out in the darkness. Other than that, it's suspiciously quiet and calm. Ade was planning to set off the fire alarm to lure the bugs back to base. She obviously managed it, as it did the job, but they've got it switched off and things back to normal super-fast. I hope she's OK.

'See you on the other side,' Mak whispers, and then he disappears into the darkness like a pro. Our group feels small without him and Ade, but Kat, Karim and I got in yesterday, so we can do it again today.

We time it so that the guards have moved out of sight, then Kat scales the wall to the broken window in just a few seconds. I don't know how someone can be so strong and light as air at the same time, but she's got it down without even looking like she's trying. If we get through this, I might see if she'll come to the climbing centre with me and try to teach me some skills. I'll probably be rubbish, but it'll be fun anyway. A minute later, she opens the door for us and we sneak inside.

'Good luck,' she whispers, hugging us both, and then she's out the door, closing it gently behind her. She'll be on the roof before we're halfway up the corridor. The lights flick on as we walk, and I realise how hard it's gonna be for Karim to get up to his mum's office without being stopped. The lights give away our location at every step, and we're so exposed.

'Karim,' I say. 'I'm going to get into the central hub and create the diversion. Whatever happens, you have to get to that office.'

'I know,' he says. 'But don't do anything dangerous.'

I stop walking and turn to him. 'Seriously, man, whatever you hear, it's all part of the plan. Promise me you'll keep going and get into your mum's computer. We have to get the XGen back on. No pressure.'

'I promise,' he says. 'I can get into her computer easy, and I'm sure I can find my way around the XGen software. You can trust me.'

'I have no doubt,' I smile. And I don't. My part is simple compared to his, or Kat's or Mak's. Simple, but not easy.

'Wait for one minute after I go through the door,' I say. 'Then get up there as fast as you can without getting caught.'

He nods. 'If you see my mum, shove some brownies in her mouth, will you?'

I give him one last smile, pull open the door to the stairwell, and run. This is it now, the only way to get all the sporelings together and away from Karim is by giving them an opportunity that they won't be able to pass up. I'm down the stairs in twenty seconds, and as I open the door, that god-awful stink whams me in the face. It's so hot in the building after days of them blasting the heating as high as it will go. The air is beyond ripe, and there's no moisture anywhere, except for the sweat that's pouring down my back and soaking through my hoody. As I turn towards the spoke that leads to the hub, I see that the lights are on in the centre of the building. They must be there, protecting the queen.

I've thought through a bunch of different ways of sneaking around and distracting the sporelings, but every one of them seemed likely to fail. I need to give my friends the time and space to do what they need to do, or all of us are doomed. So instead of hiding, or creeping, or running, I walk slowly into the hub. I walk like I'm supposed to be there. I walk with swag. And I make it almost all the way to the centre before everything goes crazy.

The hundred-metre Christmas tree is still standing. The smashed ornaments have been cleared away, and at its base, between piles of perfectly wrapped fake presents, is a desk and chair. The ring of bugs around it blocks my view, but I can see that someone is sitting there, surrounded by specimen jars, and a microscope. There must be twenty sporelings forming a protective circle around the desk, plus I see more climbing the walls and patrolling the circular balconies. They're all guarding whoever is sitting there. The queen.

As I move towards the desk, a sporeling drops to the ground in front of me from somewhere on the ceiling. He's joined almost instantly by four more – one either side and two behind me. And every bug in the room turns towards me, making the hoching sound that means I'm about ten seconds away from being bombarded with sedative spit missiles.

'Hold,' comes a voice from the desk. I hear the chair scrape, and the circle of guards parts to let the queen through. And it isn't Hoche, but it is someone I've met before – six months ago when our coach was stopped on its way into the crater. It's the person whose notes helped us to defeat the sporelings the first time around.

'Dale,' I say. 'Gotta admit, I wasn't expecting it to be you.' I smack myself in the forehead. 'The logo on the hoody in Karim's mum's office – I knew I'd seen it before. It's from the University of Nottingham. It was on your ID that we found at Crater Lake.'

'Dale was my human name,' Dale says. 'I am the leader of the hive mind, and I've been very much looking forward to talking to you.'

'I'd love to say the same, but to be honest, I would much prefer not to be having this conversation.'

'You have proved yourself to be an interesting adversary – clever, resourceful and brave. We thought we had you a couple of times, but you've eluded us. And now here you are, which makes me wonder why.' He tilts his head and stares me down.

'You want me to tell you my plan?' I say. 'Cos I don't think that's how this works. I don't know how many movies you've watched, but this is the bit when you tell me your plan, and then I escape and use it against you.'

He smiles. 'You already know my plan, you're here to try to stop it. The question is how.' He nods at the bugs behind me, and they rip the bag from my back and start searching it. They pull out a spray can, a bottle of water and a walkie-talkie.

'I assume there are tardigrades in the water,' Dale says. 'Such fascinating and enraging creatures but harmless unless they are taken into the body. What were you going to do? Contaminate my drink?' He laughs. 'And your radio waves can only disrupt our signal, they cannot damage us. My workers have been busy for weeks, dismantling XGen beacons all over town under cover of darkness. This is hardly a challenge.' He takes the walkie from the guard and drops it onto the floor, then smashes it with the heel of his shoe. I do my best to look gutted. I mean, I am a bit cos I wanted to use it to contact Ade, but it's not like I thought I'd be able to take down the whole swarm with it.

'The polymers are an annoyance, too, but you're too late to stop the galls from blooming.' Dale steps back, and one of the guards puts the water, spray can and walkie pieces in a clear plastic box like the ones in the lab. He clicks it shut and puts it on the desk.

'So, what to do with our greatest enemy?' Dale paces back and forth in front of me. 'Death by sting, perhaps.'

'What happened to you, Dale? I thought everyone was tardigraded back after Crater Lake.'

'Oh, I was,' he says. 'Stripped of my superior mind, physical strength and speed, and every other glorious thing that went along with being part of the swarm.'

'So you deliberately got yourself turned back? Weren't you only a worker, though?'

'The human I was before I evolved was set against my species. As a scientist, he was sent to work at the crater, once the spores had been murdered, to study the effects the spores had on the area. He spent a lot of time there, among the trees.'

'Right, I see how it happened,' I say.

'Such a prolonged exposure to…'

'I said I get it,' I interrupt. 'You don't need to bore on with your bugsplaining.'

He looks so mad. It's great.

'As the first of the new evolution, it was my job to build the swarm so that we can eradicate vile humans like you.'

'So you started working at Straybridge University because Straybridge won the XGen investment. You wanted to make XGen look like a sack of trash so that other towns wouldn't use it, because the signal messes with your hive mind. You probably also wanted revenge on me and my friends because we kicked your waspy butts last time. You worked your way up to Chief Science Officer so that you'd have the power to carry out your plan. Then you started bringing the trees into Straybridge, and faked the explosion at the lab, which was kind of obvious because there was no real damage, the sprinklers didn't go off, and nobody was hurt. Did you generate some kind of sonic boom?'

He opens his mouth to speak.

'No, wait, don't tell me. I don't care. With the

story about the escaped test creature, who happened to be Digger, and who you released to do your dirty work, you could keep everyone tucked up inside so you could go about your business while more and more people transformed into creepy bugs like you. Blah, blah, blah.'

He is fuming, now.

'Sorry, did I steal your moment?' I smile, cos even though I'm in a load of danger, this is a bit fun.

'Enough of this,' Dale barks. 'As much as I would enjoy watching you die, I have to acknowledge that your brain would be a valuable addition to the hive mind.'

'You must be thinking of someone else,' I say. 'I failed my last maths assessment, by a lot.'

'So...'

'I mean literally, like, I got twelve out of fifty.'

'You...'

'Also did pretty bad in art. I said it through primary, and I'm still saying it now: drawing is not a skill I possess. I just can't do it.'

He opens his mouth to speak again, so I just carry on.

'I'm average in geography, though. Just about getting through that.'

'SILENCE!' Dale yells, his face burning red.

'Man, I've never been good at listening to people who tell me to be silent. It's my human right to decide when I should be quiet and when I need to speak up.'

'Then we'll make you a lot less human,' Dale shouts. Then he hoches furiously, his mouth widening, lips pulling back to reveal a gaping hole. His mandibles shoot out like he's been doing it all his life, and then the spit ball comes flying. The guards are holding me, so I can't run, or duck. There's no escaping this one.

It thuds into my neck – warm and oozy and honestly totally disgusting. 'Gross.' I use the bottom of one of the guards' jumpers to wipe it off, but before I've even finished, I feel my eyelids drooping.

'You could have sent anyone here, but you chose to come yourself,' Dale says. 'I thought you were a leader, but you have allowed me to take advantage of your weakness.'

'That's the difference between you, and us.' I say, my mind and body shutting down at an alarming speed. 'Apparently, as a leader, you're to be protected at all costs, and you'd let others die so that you can live on. Where I come from, no one person is more important than another. No life is worth more than the rest. If I have to give mine so that my friends can survive, I'll take it. Just like they would for me.'

'And that's why you'll lose,' he laughs.

'No,' I manage to slur, though my lips feel like they belong to someone else. 'That's why we'll win.'

And, as much as I fight the sleep that's overpowering me, half a second later I sink into darkness, and I know it's game over.

24
My Squad

It takes me a moment. It's like I'm awake in my brain but not in my body, like it's rebooting – the screen frozen while the waiting circle goes round and round and round. Processing, buffering, trying to remember how it's supposed to function. And it's good in a way, cos it gives me time to think before I open my eyes.

First, I don't think I'm a bug. I don't feel any different. My body is as tired as it was before – definitely not bursting with super-strength and energy. I don't know what it's like to be part of the hive mind – do you hear voices? Do you see through other bugs' eyes? Or do you just know what the rest of them know? Whichever one it is, I don't have it. I also have the reassuring feeling of desperately wanting to punch Dale in his bug face, and that has got to be a good sign. The relief I feel is freaking huge. Thank god for the tardibrownies.

Second, I need to work out where I am and how long I've been asleep. It's boiling hot, whatever I'm lying on is hard and smooth and I can hear Dale's voice. I think I'm exactly where I fell, which is also good. I stay as still as I can, and try to keep my breathing normal.

'If he continues to suffer from his condition, he will wake soon,' a familiar voice says. Mum. 'As a new sporeling it is unlikely that his body will have had time to fully benefit from the transformation.'

'Yes, that will come later,' Dale says. 'We will wait a few minutes to be sure, and then wake him and access his mind.'

Have you ever tried pretending to be asleep? It's so much harder than it sounds. Suddenly your legs want to twitch, and your nose is itchy, and the funniest memory jumps into your mind and it's all you can do not to laugh.

'Have you found any of the others?' Dale asks, and I swear my heart stops, waiting to hear the answer.

'Not so far,' a familiar voice answers. 'But it is just a matter of time, especially when we have added the boy to the hive mind. Karim will be close.'

It's Karim's mum. And the good news is that if she's here, she's not in her office.

OK, next steps. As soon as they wake me, they'll know I'm not one of them. When that happens, they'll be raging, and most likely want to kill me. So I have a tiny window for action. I can feel the lump in my sock that means they haven't found my secret stash. That's good. I can only be maybe four metres from the tree, but that's four metres of super-strong alien parasites. I'm hoping Karim and Kat will have the XGen functioning again soon, but I need a back-up plan, just in case.

Then I hear something I don't expect. A crackle of radio static, and Karim's voice echoing across the hub. 'This is FreshTrim101 sliding into your frequency. If you can hear me, StarshottA51, now is the moment. Go!'

And I don't know what the hell is going on, but the bugs are totally silent, and the radio is crackling, so I open my eyes to see they're glitching – every one of them. Mum and Mrs Amrani are staring down at me, their eyes narrowed. Best buds, even as aliens. And standing by the main entrance door, holding a walkie-talkie in the air is someone that I'm really happy to see.

'VenomAde!' I jump up.

'Hey!' she grins. 'Looks like we're on track. You'd better do what you need to do. I don't know how long this will keep them glitching.'

With the crackling of the radio the only sound, I turn to the tree. I can get this done. I weave between the sporelings blocking my path while they stand, unmoving, apparently not even aware of what I'm doing. There are hundreds of them – all come to the hub to watch me turn. Which is exactly what I wanted.

I look around the base of the tree for the best place. Despite what some people think, this is not something I'm experienced in. Mak gave me some tips, but I'm still worried that I'll mess it up. I crouch down to pull the firelighters from my socks, at the same time as the ceiling above me crashes inwards in an explosion of glass, and with a bang so loud it shakes the walls.

I cover my head with my arms as shards rain down on me, shattering on the floor at my feet. Ade calls out, 'Starshott, enemy at twelve o'clock! On the tree!' and I look up to see Digger perched at the top of the Christmas tree, his wings flapping and antennae twitching. He's huge –

probably more than two metres tall, not including his antennae. His body has become more wasp-like – his lower half elongated and his arms and legs slimmer and encased in shiny black armour. His eyes have grown enormous, and bulge out of his face, while his nose has flattened out so much I can hardly see it. There's not really anything human about him anymore.

'He's not glitching,' I shout. 'Why isn't he glitching?'

'He's an older version of the sporelings,' Ade calls back. 'He's not part of the hive mind, so there's no signal to block.' She clicks on the walkie while Digger squats on the highest branches, like an ugly-ass fairy, clacking his mandibles and surveying the room. 'What's your status, FreshTrim?' Ade whispers into the radio.

'Logged in, just waiting on updates,' Karim says. 'How about you, KittyGrime?'

'Almost there,' Kat says. 'Two minutes.'

'Hate to rush you, guys.' Ade takes a step further away from the tree, as Digger turns to stare at her. 'But we have company.'

'What kind of company?' Karim's voice crackles.

Before Ade can answer, Digger screeches, and flings himself in her direction, his wings vibrating as he swoops towards her. She screams and leaps sideways, her finger on the button of the walkie-talkie. 'MakKarnage, we need urgent help in the hub.'

Digger roars as he misses her, and hits the first-floor balcony hard. He grips on, shakes himself, then turns to look for Ade again. He knows the radio is glitching the bugs so he's trying to take it out. 'Ade, take cover!' I shout, as Digger launches into the air for another attack.

'Hey, Digger!' I hear a voice call from the entrance. 'MakKarnage is back in the game!' Mak waves his radio in the air, and gives Ade a chance to duck and roll away from Digger's arms. Digger skids across the floor, sending glass flying in every direction.

'Remember me?' Kat's voice shouts from above me. I look up to see her leap from the frame of the roof, onto the tree. 'KittyGrime. I glued you to the climbing wall at Crater Lake.'

Digger looks from Ade, to Mak, to Kat and then scuttles across the floor towards where I'm standing at the base of the tree. I dive behind the pile of presents and he roars in frustration. Then he starts to climb the tree.

'Do it, Lance!' Kat calls down. 'We'll distract him.'

And I want to help my friends, who are fighting the most horrifying creature I've ever seen and in more danger than they've ever been before. But I know we need to finish the job, so I push the boxes up against the trunk and the lower branches, and place the firelighters among the ribbon stuff they have around them.

'You need to get clear, Kat!' I yell.

'On it,' she calls back. 'Don't wait!'

I do wait, just for a second, to watch her make an impossible jump from the tree to the second-floor balcony. She falls for half a second, and my heart lurches in my chest, but then she grips the edge with her fingers and pulls herself over the barrier. And then I take the power lighter out of my pocket, and I light up the tree.

Nothing happens, and for a moment I think the flames aren't catching. I look around for something to help the fire to stick, but as a breeze blows in through the shattered ceiling, I see wisps of smoke start to rise, and then orange flames licking over the shiny gift wrap.

'It's working!' I shout, watching as the flames grow and start to tickle the lower branches of the tree. It's been so hot in here, that even with its root ball feeding it moisture, the tree has dried out like my mum's chicken, and the fire takes hold fast.

I hear a crash over the crackling of the flames, and turn to see Ade on the floor, with Digger pinning her to the ground, crushing the walkie in his mandibles. I run to help at the same time as Kat drops from the balcony onto Digger's back. He rears up like an angry bull and tries to shake her, but she clings on around his shoulders, and stabs something into his eye. He shrieks and tries to get airborne, managing to rise a few metres above the ground, his powerful wings dislodging Kat and sending her crashing down. Then he turns to Mak, who is holding the last walkie, and speeds towards him, his eye dripping black goo. Mak doesn't have many options, and he knows he needs to protect the walkie, so he zig-zags across the hub, using anything he can to hide behind as the spit balls fly. And that's mostly glitching sporelings.

I grab the plastic box from the desk and tip it open, snatching up the bottle of water. The heat from the fire is growing fierce now, blasting out from the tree, and sweat is pouring off every bit of my skin.

'Mak!' I shout. 'Bait him, I'm coming.'

'Got it!' he calls back, and he darts toward the lift at the back of the hub where there are fewer sporelings. Digger sees his opportunity and beats his wings, rising until he's almost at the ceiling, and then he plummets towards Mak. I run.

He grabs Mak with his claw hands and tries to lift him into the air. Mak only has one free hand, but he uses it to fight, punching upwards into the joint of Digger's arm, making it buckle. Mak drops, and as Digger swoops again to catch him, I take a flying leap with my open bottle of water and throw the contents into the wound on Digger's eye. Mak hits the ground, and rolls into a crouch, while I just smack down like a brick off a bridge, and crack my chin on the rock-hard floor. Digger flails around, screeching, and swiping at his eye, then he backs away, crawls up the wall and disappears out of the broken ceiling.

'Are you OK, Lance?' Kat says, holding out a hand to help me up. 'You're bleeding again.'

'Yeah,' I say, not even bothering to wipe the

sticky wetness on my face. 'Are you? Are the others? You need to be ready to get out.'

'All good.' Ade and Mak run over.

'And we're not getting out without you,' says Kat, starting to cough. 'How long until the sprinklers kick in?'

'Anytime now would be good,' I say. And right on cue, the fire alarm goes off, followed a few seconds later by powerful sprays of water from the sprinklers around the room. The water hisses as it makes contact with the flames, the tree, and the boiling floor, dampening down the fire and releasing clouds of steam.

'Thank god,' I say. 'I know I have a reputation for being a bad-ass, but I am so not ready to go to prison for arson.'

'It's working,' Ade says. 'The fire's almost out.'

And we're so busy watching the dying flames that I don't notice the unglitching until a familiar hand grips my shoulder like a vice.

25
Humansplaining

'You could have been such an asset,' Mum says as she marches me over to where Dale stands dripping in the centre of the room. Other bugs grab Kat, Mak and Ade, and we're all lined up like we're facing a firing squad. The sprinklers spray on, drenching everything and everyone.

'What happened to the walkie?' I ask Mak.

'Battery ran out,' he says. 'Zuzie must have been using them to play crocodile hunter again. Sorry.'

'Doesn't matter,' I say. 'Maybe it's even better this way.'

'You all seem unconcerned that your plan has failed,' Dale says. 'As it seems impossible to turn you…'

'Tardibrownies.' Ade grins.

'…we'll have to end you. It's a shame. We don't like to waste host bodies, but you cannot be allowed to continue to hinder us.'

The sprinklers come to a sudden stop, but the steam still rises, swirling around us like a scene from a ghost movie. And I hope to hell this has worked, otherwise this really is the start of the end of the world.

'So when you say "end," I say, 'I assume you have something specific and disturbing in mind.'

'The sting.' Mum smiles.

'Right,' I nod. 'So it's poisonous?'

'A deadlier toxin than any other on your, or should I say *our* planet,' Dale smiles, and he looks so smug I want to smack him in the mouth.

'Will you be doing the honours?' I ask him. 'Won't you rip your smart trousers?'

'I wouldn't call them smart,' Kat says. 'No offence, Dale, but the water seems to have done something funny to the material.'

'It's sort of shrunk around your legs, and belly,' says Mak.

'Not very flattering,' Ade says. 'No offence.'

'I'm going to enjoy this,' Dale says, and he bends his knees slightly. Then nothing. He makes a confused face, straightens up, and then bends again, gritting his teeth.

I bite my lip to stop myself from laughing out of

my mouth, but a snort comes from my nose instead. I hear a giggle from Kat, and then that's it – we all start to laugh really, properly hard.

'You look like you're trying to get a tricky poo out, Dale,' I say. 'No offence.'

'I … I don't understand what's happening.'

'Would you like me to explain?' I say, then without waiting for him to answer, 'OK, you've twisted my arm.' I push my hair back to stop it dripping down my forehead. 'Well, as you know, we set your tree on fire, and when the sprinklers put it out, you thought we'd failed. But it was never the fire we wanted. While I was in here distracting you, Mak was filling the external water supply to the sprinklers with a butt-load of tardigrades. I gave myself up to get all of you inside this room, then I set the fire knowing that the sprinkler system would be activated by the heat.'

'But the water is on our skin,' Dale says. 'It hasn't been consumed. Any reaction to the tardigrades will be minor and temporary.'

'Yes, the water didn't get inside your bodies,' I say. 'But a lot of it evaporated and became steam. Our tardigrade friends are being carried by that steam. The steam you've been inhaling.'

'What?' Dale puts his hand over his nose and mouth.

'Too late for that,' Mak says. 'You already can't get your stinger out – I reckon the mandibles will be next.'

'No,' he says, but I can see that he knows it's true. He's changing – becoming human again.

Light suddenly blasts out above us, and I look up to see the candles on the roof shining white like beautiful beacons of hope and goodness.

'Karim's done it!' I say. I turn to Dale. 'You're going to glitch now, but don't worry, you'll unglitch when you're human again. Take care.'

He doesn't answer, because he's frozen with a look of complete and utter guttedness on his face.

'See you soon, Mum.' I put my hand on her shoulder and give her a sad smile, even though I know she can't see me. 'Let's wait outside,' I say. We turn to the exit.

'Hey guys, what the hell have you done to this room?' Karim comes running out of the stairwell. 'My mum is going to be raging when she debugs.'

He jogs over and grins. 'Gotta say, I'm pretty happy to be the only one here who isn't soaking wet. Or bleeding.'

'You're a legend.' I put my arm around him. 'Getting the XGen back on. The least I can do is hug you.' And I give him a massive bro hug.

'No!' he says. 'Stop!'

'Group hug moment for sure,' Kat smiles, and we all pile on, making sure that we soak Karim so he doesn't feel left out.

'Guys!' he mumbles from the middle of the huddle. 'My hair!'

26
Worth Fighting For

As Christmas days go, it's a weird one. Instead of being at home with Mum, stuffing my face with food while I open presents in the lounge, I'm in a proper nice hotel room with Mum, stuffing my face with food while I open presents in front of the TV.

'We're now going to Vanya Hoche, local journalist, and survivor of the Straybridge Invasion, reporting live from outside the town cordon.'

I groan through a mouthful of chocolate orange. 'Feels like I'm doomed to have Hoche in my life forever.'

'She helped you, though, didn't she?' Mum says, buttering her croissant.

'Maybe,' I say. 'She distracted the sporelings by tripping over, so we could get into the Cake, and gave us information we really needed. It was probably an accident, though.'

'You think she tripped over accidentally? Really?' Mum says. 'Vanya Hoche can handle her heels like no one else I've ever met. If she tripped over, it wasn't an accident.'

'Even if she was trying to help us,' I huff. 'She didn't do much. We all did way more. And Karim was the one who got us access to the labs and all the XGen stuff.'

'You know, Vanya Hoche was the one who introduced me to Nadia in the first place. If it wasn't for her, you two might not be such great friends.'

'What?'

'I was in the hospital having treatment. Nadia was there talking to the hospital about how XGen would work with their systems, and Vanya Hoche was covering a story about something or other. She brought Nadia over to me and told us we both had boys starting in Year Seven at Latham.'

I swallow my chocolate. 'No way. It's like she planned it so Karim and I would meet.'

'Hmm.' Mum lifts her croissant to her mouth. 'Perhaps she's been helping you all along.'

And that just doesn't sit right with me. Hoche is the last person in the world that I want to feel thankful for – she's an evil control freak and she made my life at Montmorency miserable. But it can't all be a coincidence; she must have known what she was doing. Just goes to show that people can always surprise you, I suppose. Everyone has good and bad in them, and she's obviously mostly bad, but maybe there's a bit of good there, too.

'Of course, we cannot go beyond the cordon,' Hoche is saying. 'Officials want to ensure the area has been fully cleansed of the contaminants that affected the residents of Straybridge before they allow people back into their homes.'

'And is there any update on what caused the outbreak?' the studio newsreader asks.

'The official line is that the accident at the university laboratories released some kind of toxin into the local area. However, it has been stressed that the accident was completely unrelated to the groundbreaking work that XGen have been undertaking in Straybridge. As soon as the area has been confirmed to be safe, the SMARTtown project will continue as planned.'

'And have they recaptured the missing test subject that also escaped in the explosion?'

'There's been no word on that specifically, but we

have received full assurances that Straybridge will be re-opened in a few days, and will be one hundred per cent safe.'

There's a knock on the door, and I jump up to open it. I'd usually still be in my pyjamas this early in the morning, but today we have plans, so I'm dressed in the new stuff Mum got me for Christmas and looking alright, apart from the scabby cuts on my cheek and chin.

'Merry Christmas!' Kat hugs me. She looks so much better, even with the rainbow of bruises on her face. For a few days after the battle at the Cake, we all struggled to sleep. You can't just shake off that worry that if you close your eyes, everything will change. But eventually we were so tired that we had to sleep, and now it's a bit easier, although I'm not sure it will ever be totally normal again.

I stand back so she can walk into our room, which is actually more like a whole house. Everyone in Straybridge was sent to nearby hotels while they remove all the 'contaminants' from town, and we lucked out with the poshest suites.

'Happy Christmas, Lance.' Ade follows after Kat. She looks more like the old Ade now, although she kept a few of the changes. They suit her, though, and she seems happier than I've seen her for months. It turns out that Kat used one of Ade's massive gold hoop earrings to stab Digger in the eye, so they played their part, even if they did make her look like a pirate.

'Mate.' Mak bumps knuckles with me. Luckily his earring seems to be gone forever, and he hasn't been moping about Georgia-Rae at all. Actually, he's been spending lots of time with Ade, which Kat is way excited about.

'Any news on the annex?' I say.

'They finally persuaded Trent to come out of the bunker.' Mak laughs. 'Apparently Madison was so mad that he left her behind that she logged onto his Xbox, sold all his skins and messed up his stats. He's fuming. We'll have to look out for him next time we play squads because I still wanna kill him.'

'Madison is my new hero,' I say.

I'm about to close the door when I hear familiar laughter down the corridor. I step out to see Karim and Chets walking together, obviously finding something hilarious.

'Lance.' Chets beams at me. 'I was just telling

Karim about that time in Year Three when you called Miss Havistock "mum" in front of the class, and Mak laughed so hard he fell off his chair.'

'Great,' I say, wondering if I'm going to regret trying to get Karim and Chets to be friends.

Karim high fives me as he bounces past. 'Tell me more, Chets,' he says. 'I need to know everything embarrassing that Lance has ever done.'

Karim's parents turn up next, all dressed up in festive jumpers, and carrying bags full of presents and food. Karim's mum puts her hand on my cheek in a reassuringly non-bug-like way, and smiles. 'Merry Christmas, Lance. Is your mum inside?' I nod, and smile back, and let them in, knowing my mum is gonna be stoked to see them.

I close the door and walk into the seating area of our room, stopping to watch everyone for a minute. Not in a creepy way, it's just honestly the best feeling in the world to see them here, and happy, and together. Life has been crazy since the summer, and there have been times when I genuinely didn't think we'd make it through. But here we are. I guess life will always throw change at you, and there will be times when people have to go their own way for a while. But knowing that I have people in my life who will always be there when it really matters makes me feel like I can face anything.

'Come on, Lance. I saved you a space,' Kat calls over, so I walk to where she's sitting, and squeeze onto the sofa next to her. She smells like apple pie, and her eyes look like something Elsa has magicked up out of the most perfect animated ice.

'Isn't this the best?' she whispers, smiling around at everyone.

'Worth fighting an alien wasp creature for?'

'Actually, yeah,' she says. 'If that doesn't sound insane?'

'Nah,' I smile. 'I know exactly what you mean.'

Acknowledgements

Writing this book was a very different experience from my previous ones, because it took place during lockdown. Some things were the same. I got the best support and encouragement from my agent, Kirsty McLachlan, who has stuck with me through years of ups and downs. I'm so looking forward to meeting in the outside world again so that I can thank you in person. My publishing team at Firefly Press has been a dream to work with. I'm really grateful to everyone at Firefly, but especially to Penny Thomas, Simone Greenwood, and Megan Farr, who work so hard for me and my books. And I absolutely love my cover, by the ridiculously talented Anne Glenn, and the beautiful map drawn by Guy Manning. I feel so lucky to have such wonderful people working with me.

There were people who cheered me on from afar, giving me the confidence to write, and to keep writing. I'm so grateful to authors Lorraine Gregory, Eloise Williams, Vanessa Harbour, Jo Clarke, and BB Taylor. I'm incredibly touched that while continuing to do their jobs brilliantly under the most difficult circumstances, so many teachers still found the time to read and share my books. Special thanks to teachers and friends Les Hall, Laura Reid, Bruce McInnes, Jane Clapp, Laura Baxter, Tami Wylie, Matthew Girvan, Sophie Topliss, Linda Canning, Jenny Caddick, Ian Hunt and Dean Boddington. I'm also grateful to the teachers who really embraced *Crater Lake* and have done loads to support it, especially Rich Simpson and Nick Turley. The support of bloggers Kate Poels, Liam (@notsotweets), Jo (@BookSuperhero2), and Amy (@GoldenBooksGirl) has been such a boost. I am thankful for all the brilliant librarians and booksellers who work with such passion and knowledge to get books into the hands of children; and I am especially grateful to Bronnie and Bob at Bookwagon for all they do. I also have to say an enormous thank you to Book Trust, who have supported me from the start, and who gave *Crater Lake* an amazing opportunity by choosing it to be part of Bookbuzz.

I owe a special thank you to three children who were kind enough to read and review *Evolution* before it came out: Michael Chen, Louise Chen, and Emily Edge, you are all superstars.

Thanks to my good friends Emma Savin, Nicola Wareing, Laura Endersby, and Sarah Hill. I can't wait to see you, and hug you, and buy you all a drink. And to Mum, Dad, Julie and Alfie, and David – thank you for your support. I miss you all so much.

To the people who were stuck with me while I tried to get *Evolution* written, I owe the biggest thank you. I couldn't have done this without my husband Dean, who helped me with the science, the plot, the puns, and a million other daily things. I am so lucky to have five beautiful children who are all smart, funny, and kind people in their different ways. Stanley, Teddy, Mia, Helena, and Luis: you inspire me every day. Never change.

Crater Lake introduced me to more new readers than I ever thought I'd have, and I've been moved to tears by some of the reviews, messages and *Crater Lake* inspired creations that I've seen and received. So to every reader who has gasped, jumped or laughed along with Lance, Kat, Chets, Mak, and Ade: I hope this second instalment is everything you wanted it to be. Thank you for reading, and I hope you don't have nightmares.